Bert Wilson's Fadeaway Ball

By

J. W. Duffield

Bert Wilson's Fadeaway Ball

CHAPTER I

TOUCHING SECOND

Crack!—and the ball soared into center field, while the batter, swift as a flash, sped down to first. A tremendous roar went up from the thirty thousand loyal "fans" who packed the grandstands and filled the bleachers to overflowing. Staid citizens danced up and down like howling dervishes, hats were tossed into the air or jovially crushed on their owners' heads, and happy riot reigned everywhere. Pandemonium broke loose.

The fight for the pennant had been a bitter one all season. First one team and then another had taken the lead, while the whole country had been as excited as though the fate of an empire hung in the balance. The third chief contender, fighting grimly to the last, had fallen hopelessly behind, and the contest had narrowed down to a life-and-death struggle between the Giants and the Cubs. The team from the Western city had hung on doggedly and every battle had been fought "for blood." Contesting every inch, they had at last drawn up on even terms with the leaders, and to-day's game was to decide which club should be hailed as champions of the National League and, later on, do battle with the leaders of the American League for the proud title of Champions of the World.

The excitement was intense, and, to a foreigner, would have been inconceivable. Men stood in line all the night before to make sure of tickets when the gates should open in the morning. The newspapers devoted columns of space to the gladiators of the opposing teams. Delegations poured in on special trains from neighboring cities. The surface cars and elevated trains, packed to the limit, rolled up to the grounds and deposited their sweltering throngs. The lines of ticket buyers extended for blocks, and the speculators did a rushing business. Long before the hour set for the game to begin, the grounds were crowded to suffocation, and thousands, unable to get in, were turned away from the gates.

The scene within was inspiring. A band played popular airs, while those within hearing joined lustily in the chorus. The great field, gleaming like green velvet beneath the afternoon sun, had been especially groomed and rolled for this day of days. The base lines, freshly marked, stood out in white and dazzling relief. All four sides of the huge enclosure held their thousands of enthusiasts, and the host of special policemen had their hands full to keep them from encroaching on the diamond. As each white-uniformed athlete of the home team came from the club house for preliminary practice, he was boisterously and affectionately greeted.

Nor did the gray-clad visitors come short of a cordial reception. The great crowd hoped that the home team would win, but they were fair, and, mingled with the good-natured chaffing, was a wholesome respect and fear of their prowess. Above all they wanted a rattling game and a hair-raising finish, with the Giants winning "by an eyelash."

The bell rang. The Giants took their places in the field and the umpire cried "Play ball!" The head of the Cubs' batting order came to the plate and the game was on. From the start it was a battle "for keeps." Both teams were "on their toes." It meant not only honor but lucre. The winners would contest in the World's Series, and this meant thousands of dollars for every player. Every point was bitterly fought, and plays were made that under other circumstances would not even have been attempted. For eight innings, Fortune divided her favors equally, and it looked as though the game were destined to go into extra innings.

The Cubs were easily disposed of in their half of the ninth, and the Giants came to the bat. The crowd, which had been alternately on the heights of hope or in the depths of despair, rose to their feet and cheered them wildly. The batters were frantically besought to "hit it on the seam," "give the ball a ride," "show them where you live." The players responded nobly. By the time that two were out, a Giant was perched on third and another on first. The shortstop, a sure hitter in a pinch, strode to the plate. Now, indeed, excitement was at fever heat. A safe hit into the outfield would bring the man on third to the plate with the winning run.

The visitors were plainly worried. The "Peerless Leader" came in from first, ostensibly to advise the pitcher, but really to give him a moment's rest before the final test. Hoots of derision showed the spectators' appreciation of the trick. The pitcher glanced at the man dancing about third, wound up deliberately and let the ball go with all the force of his brawny arm. The batter caught it squarely "on the trademark" and shot it like a rifle bullet into center field, while the man on third tore down the line and came like a racehorse to the plate. He crossed the rubber with the winning run, and thirty thousand men went stark, raving mad.

The man on first ran part way toward second, and then, seeing that his comrade would certainly score, turned and scurried to the club house in right field. The jubilant crowd began to invade the diamond. Suddenly the second baseman of the visitors secured the ball, rushed to his base, and then, surrounded by his teammates, ran toward the umpire, waving his hands wildly.

The crowd, at first bewildered, then angered, soon became panic-stricken. Few of them understood the nature of the claim. They only felt that the hard-won victory was being called in question, and a tidal wave of wrath and resentment swept over the field.

The point made by the quick-witted second baseman was simple, but sufficiently important to engage the grave attention of the umpires. His contention was that the man on first had not touched second base, and, as he was legally compelled to leave first in order to make room for the batter and had not touched second before the ball got there, he was forced out, and therefore the run didn't count. The rules on this point were clear and explicit. If the claim was granted, three men were out, no run had come in and the score was still a tie at one to one.

The final decision was held in suspense, and the throng passed out, more like a funeral than a triumphal procession. Disputes were rife among heated partisans, and in all the vast city that night and, in a lesser degree, in every city from New York to San Francisco, the game was fought over and over again. The unfortunate first baseman almost lost his mind over the blunder. There was more pity than bitterness felt toward him, however, as it was known that he had merely followed a general custom that had been taken as a matter of course.

Among the crowd that filed out of the gates were Bert Wilson and his inseparable friends, Dick Trent and Tom Henderson. With them also was a Mr. Hollis, a gentleman much older than they in years, but quite as young in spirit. He had been in charge of the summer camp from which the boys had recently returned, and the respect and confidence that his sterling character evoked had become steadily stronger. They were all very fond of the great national game, and had shared the enthusiasm over the supposed victory of the home team. Now, from the reaction, their ardor was correspondingly dampened.

"There's no use talking," broke out Tom hotly, "it was a low down trick. They couldn't beat us with the bat, so they try to do it on a quibble."

"I don't know," said Dick, "it's about a stand off. We may have been a little bit better off in brawn, but they had it on us in the matter of brain. Whatever we may think of their sportsmanship, their wits were not wool gathering."

"And after all," chimed in Bert, "it is brain that counts to-day in baseball as well as in everything else. More and more, the big leaguers are putting a premium on quick thinking. The mere 'sand lot slugger' is going to the rear, and the college man is coming to the front. It isn't that the collegian is necessarily any brainier, but he has been taught how to use his brains. This is simply a case where the husky hit of the Giants' short-stop was wasted because of the nimble wit of the Cubs' second baseman. It was hit against wit, and wit won out."

"All the same," maintained Tom, "it was taking advantage of a technicality. The same thing has been done a hundred times, and there has never been a kick about it. Whenever a player has been sure that the winning run has come in, he has considered it all over, and made a break for the clubhouse. I don't think the question has ever been raised before."

"Yes it has," said Mr. Hollis. "That same quick thinker made a point of it the other day in Pittsburgh, and that is all the more reason why the home team ought to have been wide awake. But there is nothing to be gained by post mortems, and anyway the thing isn't settled yet. It looks rather bad for us now, but there will be a full discussion of the matter and the umpires may find something in the rules that will cover the case and give us the run. Even if they don't, it leaves it a tie, and the game will have to be played over. We may win then and get the pennant after all."

"I hope so," said Tom, "but just at present I know how they felt in Mudville:

"'O somewhere birds are singing and somewhere children shout,But there's no joy in Mudville—mighty Casey has struck out.'"

A few days later when the point had been decided in favor of the Cubs and the game played over, only to result in a conclusive victory for the men from the shore of Lake Michigan, the chums met in Bert's rooms.

"Well," said Dick, "I see that they put it over, all right. They've copped the pennant and we are only an 'also ran.'"

"Yes," replied Tom, "that hit by Tinker over Seymour's head did the business. But there's no use crying over spilt milk. We'll stand them on their heads next year and get even."

"By the way, Bert," asked Dick, changing the subject, "have you heard from your examinations yet? How did you make out?"

"Fine," answered Bert. "I heard from the Dean this morning and he says that I passed with something to spare. The chemical and electrical marks were especially good. He says that the questions along those lines were unusually severe, but they didn't strike me that way. I suppose it's because I'm so interested in them that they come easy."

"Good for you, old scout," cried Dick, delightedly. "I'm tickled to death that the thing is settled. You'll find that we have one of the finest scientific schools in the country. I've been there a year now, and it's come to seem like home. I'll show you the ropes and we'll room together. I only wish Tom here were coming along with us next week."

"So do I," said Tom ruefully, "but Father seems to think I'd better stick to my engineering course right here in New York. It isn't that he thinks the course is any better than at your college, if as good. I suppose the real reason is that he wants me to be where I can live at home. I'm going to get Mr. Hollis to have a talk with him. Perhaps he can show him that it would be a good thing for me to get away from home and be thrown on my own responsibility. Dad's pretty stubborn when he gets an idea in his head, but he thinks a lot of Mr. Hollis, and what he says will go a long way with him."

It was a wholesome group of young fellows that thus discussed their future plans. They were the best type of manly, red-blooded American youth, full of energy and ambition and alive to their finger tips. Tom was of medium height, while Bert and Dick were fully six feet tall. All were strongly built and looked as though they could give a good account of themselves in any contest, whether of mind or body. A similarity of tastes and habits had drawn them closely together, and among their friends they were jokingly referred to as the "Three Guardsmen." They were rarely apart, and now their plans for the coming school year were destined to cement their friendship still more firmly. In reality with them it was "one for all and all for one."

All of them had chosen their life work along practical and scientific lines. The literary professions did not tempt them strongly. Dick, who was the elder, was preparing to become a mining engineer, and had already spent a year at college with that end in view. Tom aimed at civil engineering while Bert was strongly drawn toward electrical science and research. This marvelous field had a fascination for him that he could not resist. His insight was so clear, he leaped so intuitively from cause to conclusion, that it was felt that it would be almost a crime if he were not permitted to have every advantage that the best scientific schools could give him. For a long time past he had been studying nights, preparing for his entrance examinations, and now that he had passed them triumphantly, nothing intervened between him and his cherished ambition.

Absorbed as he was in his studies, however, he spent enough time in athletic sports to keep himself in superb physical condition. His was the old Greek ideal of a "sound mind in a sound body." His favorite sport was baseball, and, like most healthy young Americans, he was intensely fond of the great game. In public school and high school he had always "made the team." Although at times he had played every position in the infield and outfield and behind the bat, he soon gravitated towards the pitcher's box, and for the last three years had played that position steadily. He was easily the best "flinger" in the Inter-Scholastic League, and had received more than one invitation to join some of the semi-professional teams that abound in the great city. He elected, however, to remain purely and simply an amateur. Even when a "big league" scout, who had watched him play, gave him a quiet tip that his club would take him on the Spring training trip to Texas and pay all his expenses, with a view to finding out whether he was really "major league timber," the offer did not tempt him. He had no idea of making a business of his chosen sport, but simply a pleasant though strenuous recreation. With him, it was "sport for sport's sake"; the healthy zest of struggle, the sheer physical delight in winning.

And now, as they talked over the coming year, the athletic feature also came to the fore.

"I wonder if I'll have the slightest show to make the baseball team," said Bert. "I suppose, as a newcomer I'll be a rank outsider."

"Don't you believe that for a minute," replied Dick warmly. "Of course there'll be lots of competition and a raft of material to pick from. I suppose when the coach sends out the call for candidates in the Spring, there'll be dozens of would-be players and a bunch too of have-beens that will trot out on the diamond to be put through their paces. One thing is certain, though, and that is that you'll get your chance. There may be a whole lot of snobbery in college life—though there isn't half as much as people think—but, out on the ball field, it's a pure democracy. The only question there is whether you can deliver the goods. If you can, they don't care whether you're a new man or an old-timer. All they want is a winner."

"Well," chimed in Tom, "they'll find that they have one in Bert. Just show them a little of the 'big medicine' you had in that last game with Newark High when you put out the side on three pitched balls. Gee, I never saw a more disgusted bunch of ball tossers. Just when they thought they had the game all sewed up and put away in their bat bag, too."

"That's all right," said Bert, "but you must remember that those high school fellows were a different proposition from a bunch of seasoned old college sluggers. When I come up against them, if I ever do, they'll probably smash the back fences with the balls I feed to them."

"Some of them certainly can slaughter a pitcher's curves," laughed Dick. "Old Pendleton, for instance, would have the nerve to start a batting rally against three-fingered Brown, and Harry Lord wouldn't be hypnotized even if Matty glared at him."

"I understand you did some fence breaking yourself last Spring on the scrubs," said Tom. "Steve Thomas told me you were the heaviest batter in college."

"O, I don't know," returned Dick modestly, "I led them in three-base hits and my batting average was .319, but Pendleton was ahead of me in the matter of home runs. I hope to do better next Spring, though, as Ainslee, the coach, gave me some valuable tips on hitting them out. At first I swung too much and tried to knock the cover off the ball. The result was that when I did hit the ball it certainly traveled some. But many a time I missed them because I took too long a swing. Ainslee showed me how to chop at the ball with a sharp, quick stroke that caught it just before the curve began to break. Then all the power of my arms and shoulders leaned up against the ball at just the right second. Ainslee says that Home-Run Baker uses that method altogether, and you know what kind of a hitter he is. I got it down pretty fine before the season ended, and if I make the team next Spring――"

"If you make it," said Bert incredulously. "As though it wasn't a dead certainty."

"Not a bit of it," protested Dick, seriously. "You never can tell from year to year. You can't live on your reputation at college. There may be a regular Hal Chase among the new recruits, and he may win the first base position over me without half trying. It's a good thing it is so, too, because we have to keep hustling all the time or see somebody else step into our shoes. The result is that when the team is finally licked into shape by the coaches, it represents the very best the college can turn out. It's a fighting machine that never knows when it is whipped and never quits trying until the last man is out in the ninth inning."

"Yes," broke in Tom, "and that's what makes college baseball so much more pleasing than the regular professional game. The fellows go at it in such deadly earnest. It is the spirit of Napoleon's Marshal: 'The Old Guard dies, but never surrenders.' The nine may be beaten, but not disgraced, and, when the game is over, the winning team always knows that it has been in a fight."

"Well," said Bert, as the fellows rose to go, "if we do make the team, it won't be through lack of trying if we fail to land the pennant."

"No," laughed Dick. "Our epitaph at least will be that of the Texas cowboy,

"'He done his blamedest—angels can no more.'"

A week later, the three friends—for Tom and Mr. Hollis had won his father over—stood on the deck of a Sound steamer, saying goodby to those who had come to see them off. Mr. Hollis wrung Bert's hand, just as the last bell rang and he prepared to go down the gangway.

"Good luck, Bert, and whatever else you do, don't forget to touch second."

He smiled at Bert's puzzled expression, and added: "I mean, my boy, be thorough in all you do. End what you begin. Don't be satisfied with any half-way work. Many a man has made a brilliant start, but a most dismal finish. In work, in play, in the whole great game of life—touch second."

CHAPTER II

"MAKING THE TEAM"

The Fall and Winter passed quickly. Bert and Dick roomed together in one of the dormitories close to the main buildings, while Tom had his quarters on the floor below. The feeling of strangeness, inevitable at the start, soon wore off, and they quickly became a part of the swarming life that made the college a little world of its own.

Here, too, as in the greater world outside, Bert found all sorts and conditions. There were the rich and the poor, the polished and the uncouth, the lazy and the energetic, good fellows and bad. But the good predominated. The great majority were fine, manly fellows, sound to the core. Dick's wide acquaintanceship with them and his familiarity with college customs were immensely helpful to Bert from the beginning, and he was soon a general favorite.

The football season had been a triumphant one, and another gridiron championship had been added to the many that had preceded it. There had been a surplus of good material left over from the year before, and the time was so short that Bert had not tried for the team. At the outset, too, his studies taxed him so heavily that he did not feel justified in giving the necessary attention to the great game, that, in his estimation, almost divided honors with baseball. He had done a little playing with the scrubs, however, and on his class team, and the qualities he displayed in "bucking the line" had marked him out to the coaches, as a factor to be reckoned with in the following seasons.

The Christmas holidays had come and gone almost before he knew it, and when he returned for his second term, he buckled down to work with all his might. His chosen field of electricity held constant surprises for him, as it became more familiar. If he had any specialty, it was wireless telegraphy. There was an irresistible attraction in the mysterious force that bound the ends of the earth together by an electric spark, that leaped over oceans with no conductor but the air, that summoned help for sinking vessels when all other hope was gone. He felt that the science was as yet only in its infancy, and that it held untold possibilities for the future. The splendidly equipped laboratories gave him every opportunity and encouragement for original work, and his professors foresaw a brilliant future for the enthusiastic young student.

Spring came early that year. A soft wind blew up from the south, the sun shone warmly on the tender grass, the sap stirred blindly in the trees. It stirred also in the veins of the lusty college youth and called them to the outdoor life.

Going down the hall, one morning, to his recitation room, Bert came across an eager group surrounding the bulletin board. He crowded nearer and saw that it was the call of the coach to baseball candidates to report on the following day. His heart leaped in response and the morrow seemed long in coming.

Dressed in the old baseball togs that had done yeoman service on many a hard-fought field, he with Dick and Tom, who were quite as eager as himself, reported for the tryout. Perhaps a hundred ambitious youngsters were on hand, all aflame with desire to make the team and fight for the glory of Alma Mater. It was apparent at a glance, however, that many had ambition but nothing else. The qualities that had made them heroes on some village nine were plainly inadequate, when it came to shaping up for a college team. The hopes of many faded away when they saw the plays made by the seasoned veterans, who nonchalantly "ate up" balls and did stunts in practice that would have called out shouts of applause in a regular game. But whether marked for acceptance or rejection, all were as frolicsome as colts turned out to pasture. It was good to be young and to be alive.

The coach threaded his way through the groups with an eye that apparently saw nothing, but, in reality, saw everything. He was a famous pitcher, known from one end of the country to the other. Himself an old-time graduate, he had the confidence of the faculty and the unbounded respect and admiration of the students. He had been given full charge and was an absolute autocrat. Whatever he said "went," and from his decision there was no appeal. He played no favorites, was not identified with any clique, and his sole desire was to duplicate the success of the preceding season and turn out a winner.

To do this, he realized, would be no easy task. While his two chief rivals had maintained their strong teams almost intact, his own was "shot to pieces." Three had graduated, and they were among his heaviest hitters. Good old Pendleton, who had been a tower of strength at first base, who could take them with equal ease to right or left and "dig them out of the dirt," and whose hard slugging had many a time turned defeat into victory, would be hard to replace. His pitching staff was none too good. Winters lacked control, and Benson's arm was apt to give out about the seventh inning. Hinsdale was a good backstop, but his throwing to second was erratic. They had done too much stealing on him last year. Barry would be sadly missed at third, and it would be mighty hard to find a capable guardian for the "difficult corner." It was clear that he faced a tough problem, and the only solution was to be found, if at all, in the new material.

As he glanced musingly around his eyes fell on Bert. They rested there. He knew a thoroughbred when he saw one, and this was undeniably a thoroughbred. The lithe form, supple as a leopard's, the fine play of shoulder muscles that the uniform could not conceal, the graceful but powerful swing, the snap with which the ball shot from his fingers as though released by a spring—all these he noticed in one practised glance. He sauntered over to where Bert was pitching.

"Done much in the pitching line?" he asked carelessly.

"A little," answered Bert modestly, "only on high school nines though."

"What have you got in stock?" asked the coach.

"Not much besides the old 'roundhouse' curve," replied Bert. "I don't think so much of my incurve, though I'm trying to make it break a little more sharply. I can do a little 'moist' flinging, too, though I haven't practised that much."

"Don't," said the coach. "Cut out the spitball. It's bound to hurt your arm in the long run. Trot out your curve and let's have a look at it. Easy now," he said as Bert wound up, "don't put too much speed in it. You'll have plenty of chances to do that later on."

The ball left Bert's hand with a jerk, and, just before it reached the center of the plate, swept in a sharp, tremendous curve to the outside, so that the catcher just touched it with the end of his fingers.

"Not so bad," commented the coach carelessly, though his eyes lighted up. "Here, Drake," he called to a burly veteran who was looking on with interest, "take your wagon tongue and straighten out this youngster's curves."

The good-natured giant, thus addressed, picked up his bat and came to the plate.

"Get it over the plate now, kid, and I'll kill it," he grinned.

A little flustered by this confidence, Bert sent one in waist high, just cutting the corner. Drake swung at it and missed it by six inches.

"One strike," laughed the coach, and Drake, looking a little sheepish, set himself for the next.

"Give him a fast one now, shoulder high," ordered the coach. Again the ball sped toward the plate and Drake struck at it after it had passed him and thudded into the catcher's glove.

"Gee, I can't hit them if I can't see them," he protested, and the coach chuckled.

"No," he said, as Bert poised himself for a third pitch, "no more just now. I don't want you to throw your arm out at practice. There are other days coming, and you won't complain of lack of work. Come out again to-morrow," and he walked away indifferently, while his heart was filled with exultation. If he had not unearthed a natural-born pitcher, he knew nothing about ball players.

Drake was more demonstrative. While Bert was putting on his sweater, he came up and clapped him on the shoulder.

"Say, Freshie," he broke out, "that was a dandy ball you whiffed me with. You certainly had me guessing. If that swift one you curled around my neck had hit me, I would have been seeing stars and hearing the birdies sing. And I nearly broke my back reaching for that curve. You've surely got something on the ball."

"Oh, you'd have got me all right, if I'd kept on," answered Bert. "That was probably just a fluke, and I was lucky enough to get away with it."

"Well, you can call it a fluke if you like," rejoined Drake, "but to me it looked suspiciously like big league pitching. Go to it, my boy, and I'll root for you to make the team."

Bert flushed with pleasure at this generous meed of praise, doubly grateful as coming from an upper class man and hero of the college diamond. Dick coming up just then, they said good-by to Drake and started toward their dormitory.

"What's this I hear about you, Bert?" asked Dick; "you've certainly made yourself solid with Ainslee. I accidentally heard him telling one of the assistant coaches that, while of course he couldn't be sure until he'd tried you out a little more, he thought he'd made a find."

"One swallow doesn't make a summer," answered Bert. "I had Drake buffaloed all right, but I only pitched two balls. He might knock me all over the lot to-morrow."

"Sufficient unto the day are the hits thereof," rejoined Dick; "the fact is that he didn't hit you, and he has the surest eye in college. If he had fouled them, even, it would have been different, but Ainslee said he missed them by a mile. And even at that you weren't at full speed, as he told you not to cut loose to-day."

"Well," said Bert, "if the lightning strikes my way, all right. But now I've got to get busy on my 'Sci' work, or I'll surely flunk to-morrow."

The next day Bert was conscious of sundry curious glances when he went out for practice. News travels fast in a college community and Drake had passed the word that Ainslee had uncovered a "phenom." But the coach had other views and was in no mood to satisfy their curiosity. He had turned the matter over in his mind the night before and resolved to bring Bert along slowly. To begin with, while delighted at the boy's showing on the first time out, he realized that this one test was by no means conclusive. He was naturally cautious. He was "from Missouri" and had to be "shown." A dozen questions had to be answered, and, until they were, he couldn't reach any definite decision. Did the boy have stamina enough to last a full game? Was that wonderful curve of his under full control? Was his heart in the right place, or, under the tremendous strain of a critical game, would he go to pieces? Above all, was he teachable, willing to acknowledge that he did not "know it all," and eager to profit by the instruction that would be handed out in the course of the training season? If all these questions could be answered to his satisfaction, he knew that the most important of all his problems—that of the pitcher's box—was already solved, and that he could devote his attention to the remaining positions on the team.

Pursuing this plan of "hastening slowly," he cut out all "circus" stunts in this second day's practice. Bert was instructed to take it easy, and confine himself only to moderately fast straight balls, in order to get the kinks out of his throwing arm. Curves were forbidden until the newness wore off and his arm was better able to stand the strain. The coach had seen too many promising young players ruined in trying to rush the season, and he did not propose to take any such chances with his new find.

His keen eyes sparkled, as from his position behind the pitcher, he noted the mastery that Bert had over the ball. He seemed to be able to put it just where he wished. Whether the coach called for a high or a low ball, straight over the center of the plate or just cutting the corners, the ball obeyed almost as though it were a living thing. Occasionally it swerved a little from the exact "groove" that it was meant to follow, but in the main, as Ainslee afterward confided to his assistant, "the ball was so tame that it ate out of his hand."

He was far too cautious to say as much to Bert. Of all the dangers that came to budding pitchers, the "swelled head" was the one he most hated and detested.

"Well," he said as he pretended to suppress a yawn, "your control is fairly good for a beginner. Of course I don't know how it will be on the curves, but we'll try them out too before long."

"That," he went on warming to his subject, "is the one thing beyond all others you want to work for. No matter how much speed you've got or how wide your curve or how sharp your break, it doesn't amount to much, unless you can put the ball where you want it to go. Of course, you don't want to put every ball over the plate. You want to make them 'bite' at the wide ones. But when you are 'in the hole,' when there are two strikes and three balls, the winning pitcher is the one that nine times out of ten can cut the plate, and do it so surely that the umpire will have no chance to call it a ball. One of the greatest pitchers I ever knew was called the 'Curveless Wonder.' He didn't have either an incurve or an outcurve that was worth mentioning. But he had terrific speed, and such absolute ability to put the ball just where he wanted it, that for years he stood right among the headliners in the major leagues. Take my word for it, Wilson, a pitcher without control is like the play of Hamlet with Hamlet left out. Don't forget that."

The respect with which Bert listened was deepened by his knowledge that Ainslee was himself famous, the country over, in this same matter of control. A few more comments on minor points, and the coach walked away to watch the practice of his infield candidates.

Now that Pendleton had graduated, the logical successor of the great first baseman seemed to be Dick Trent, who had held the same position on the scrubs the year before, and who had pressed Pendleton hard for the place. The first base tradition demands that it be occupied by a heavy batter, and there was no doubt that in this particular Dick filled the bill. His average had been well above the magic .300 figures that all players covet, and now that he had conquered his propensity to excessive swinging, he might fairly be expected to better these figures this year. As a fielder, he was a sure catch on thrown balls either to right or left, and his height and reach were a safe guarantee that not many wild ones would get by him. He was lightning quick on double plays, and always kept his head, even in the most exciting moments of the game. If he had any weakness, it was, perhaps, that he did not cover quite as deep a field as Pendleton used to, but that was something that careful coaching could correct. None of the other candidates seemed at all above the average, and, while yet keeping an open mind, the coach mentally slated Dick for the initial bag.

Second and short, as he said to himself with a sigh of relief, were practically provided for. Sterling at the keystone bag and White at shortfield were among the brightest stars of the college diamond, and together with Barry and Pendleton had formed the famous "stonewall" infield that last year had turned so many sizzling hits to outs.

Barry—ah, there was a player! A perfect terror on hard hit balls, a fielder of bunts that he had never seen excelled, even among professional players. He remembered the screeching liner that he had leaped into the air and pulled down with one hand, shooting it down to first for a double play in the last game of the season. It had broken up a batting rally and saved the game when it seemed lost beyond redemption.

Well, there were as good fish in the sea as ever were caught, and no man was so good but what another just as good could be found to take his place. But where to find him? There was the rub. That cub trying out now at third—what was his name?—he consulted the list in his hand—oh, yes, Henderson—he rather fancied his style. He certainly handled himself like a ball player. But there—you never could tell. He might simply be another "false alarm."

At this moment the batter sent a scorching grounder toward third, but a little to the left of the base. Tom flung himself toward it, knocked it down with his left hand, picked it up with the right and scarcely waiting to get "set" shot it like a flash to first. The coach gasped at the scintillating play, and White called out:

"Classy stuff, kid, classy stuff. That one certainly had whiskers on it."

"Hey, there, Henderson," yelled the coach, "go easy there. Float them down. Do you want to kill your arm with that kind of throwing?"

But to himself he said: "By George, what a 'whip' that fellow's got. That ball didn't rise three inches on the way to first. And it went into Drake knee high. That youngster will certainly bear watching."

And watch him he did with the eye of a hawk, not only that afternoon, but for several weeks thereafter until the hope became a certainty that he had found a worthy successor to the redoubtable Barry, and his infield would be as much of a "stonewall" that season as the year before. With Hodge in right, Flynn in center and Drake in left, his outfield left nothing to be desired, either from a fielding or batting point of view, and he could now devote himself entirely to the development of his batteries.

Under his masterly coaching, Bert advanced with great rapidity. He had never imagined that there was so much in the game. He learned from this past-master in the art how to keep the batter "hugging first"; the surest way of handling bunts; the quick return of the ball for the third strike before the unsuspecting batter can get "set," and a dozen other features of "inside stuff" that in a close game might easily turn the scale. Ainslee himself often toed the plate and told Bert to send in the best he had. His arm had attained its full strength, under systematic training, and he was allowed to use his curves, his drop, his rise ball and the swift, straight one that, as Flynn once said, "looked as big as a balloon when it left his hand, but the size of a pea when it crossed the plate."

One afternoon, when Ainslee had taken a hand in the batting practice, Bert fed him an outcurve, and the coach smashed it to the back fence. A straight high one that followed it met with no better fate. It was evident that Ainslee had his "batting eye" with him that afternoon, and could not be easily fooled.

"Send in the next," he taunted, good-naturedly, "I don't think you can outguess me to-day."

A little nettled at his discomfiture, Bert wound up slowly. For some time past he had been quietly trying out a new delivery that he had stumbled upon almost by accident. He called it his "freak" ball. He had thrown it one day to Dick, when, after the regular practice, they were lazily tossing the ball to and fro. It had come in way below where Dick's hands were waiting for it, and the latter was startled. It was a "lulu," he said emphatically. It could not be classed with any of the regulation curves. Bert had kept it under cover until he could get perfect control of it. Now he had got it to the point where he could put it just where he wanted it, and as he looked at the smiling face of the coach he resolved to "uncork" it.

He took a long swing and let it go. It came to the plate like a bullet, hesitated, slowed, then dropped down and in, a foot below the wild lunge that the coach made for it. His eyes bulged, and he almost dropped the bat.

"What was that?" he asked. "How did you do it? Put over another one."

A second one proved just as puzzling, and the coach, throwing his bat aside, came down to the pitcher's box. He was clearly excited.

"Now, what was it?" he asked; "it wasn't an incurve, a drop, or a straight, but a sort of combination of them all. It was a new one on me. How do you hold your hand when you throw it?"

"Why," replied Bert, "when I throw it, the palm is held toward the ground instead of toward the sky, as it is when I pitch an outcurve. The wrist is turned over and the hand held down with the thumb toward the body, so that when the ball slips off the thumb with a twisting motion it curves in toward the batter. I grip it in the same way as an outcurve. Just as it twists off the thumb I give it a sharp snap of the wrist. It spins up to the plate, goes dead, then curves sharply down and in."

"Well," said the coach, "it's certainly a dandy. We must develop it thoroughly, but we'll do it on the quiet. I rather think we'll have a surprise for 'our friends the enemy,' when the race begins. It's just as well to have an ace up our sleeve. That ball is in a class by itself. It just seems to melt while you are trying to locate it. If I were to give it a name at all, I'd call it a 'fadeaway.'"

And so Bert's new delivery was christened. As they walked back to the college both were exultant. They would have been still more so, if at that moment they had begun to realize the havoc and dismay that would be spread among their opponents before the season ended by Bert's fadeaway ball.

CHAPTER III

THE "INSIDE" GAME

"Well, Tom, I see that you lead off in the batting order," said Bert, as they sat in his rooms at the close of the day's work.

"Yes," said Tom, "Ainslee seems to think that I am a good waiter, as well as a pretty fair sprinter, and I suppose that is the reason he selected me."

"'They also serve who only stand and wait,'" recited Dick, who was always ready with an apt quotation.

"Well," laughed Bert, "I don't suppose the poet ever dreamed of that application, but, all the same, it is one of the most important things in the game to lead off with a man who has nerve and sense enough to wait. In the first place, the pitcher is apt to be a little wild at the start and finds it hard to locate the plate. I know it's an awful temptation to swing at a good one, if it is sandwiched in between a couple of wild ones, and, of course, you always stand the chance of being called out on strikes. But at that stage of the game he is more likely to put over four balls than three strikes, and if you do trot down to first, you've got three chances of reaching home. A sacrifice will take you down to second, and then with only one man out and two good batters coming up, a single to the outfield brings you home."

"Then, too, you went around the bases in fifteen seconds flat, the other day," said Dick, "and that's some running. I noticed Ainslee timing you with his split-second watch, and when he put it back in his pocket he was smiling to himself."

"Flynn comes second, I see," said Bert, consulting his list, "and that's a good thing too. He is one of the best 'place' hitters on the team. He has the faculty that made Billy Keeler famous, of 'hitting them where they ain't.' He's a dandy too at laying down a bunt, just along the third-base line. If any man can advance you to second, Flynn can."

"Yes," said Tom, "with Drake up next, swinging that old wagon tongue of his, and then Dick coming on as a clean-up hitter, it will have to be pretty nifty pitching that will keep us from denting the home plate."

"Last year the team had a general batting average of .267," chimed in Dick. "If we can match that this year, I guess there'll be no complaint. As a matter of fact, however, I'm a little dubious of doing that, especially with old Pendleton off the team. But if we come short a little there, I am counting on Bert holding down the batters on the other nines enough to make up for it."

"If I get a chance, I'll do my very best," said Bert, "but perhaps I won't pitch in a regular game all season. You know how it is with a Freshman. He may have to sit on the bench all the time, while the upper class pitchers take their turn in the box. They've won their spurs and I haven't. They've 'stood the gaff' under the strain of exciting games, and pulled victories out of the fire. I might do it too, but nobody knows that, and I probably would not be called on to go in the box, except as a last resort. They may believe that I have the curve, but they are not at all sure that I have the nerve. Winters and Benson are going along now like a house afire, and if they are at top speed when the season begins I'll see the pennant won or lost from my seat on the bench."

"Neither one of them has anything on you," maintained Tom stoutly. "Of course they are, in a certain sense, veterans, and then, too, they have the advantage of having faced before many of the players on the other teams. That counts for a lot, but you must remember that Hinsdale has caught for the last two years, and he knows these things as well as the pitchers. He knows their weak and their strong points, the ones that simply kill a low outcurve, but are as helpless as babies before a high fast one. He could quickly put you on to the batters' weakness. But outside of that you've got them faded. You have more speed than Winters and more endurance than Benson. Neither one of them has a license to beat you at any stage of the pitching game."

"Perhaps it's your friendship rather than your judgment that's talking now, Tom," smiled Bert.

"No," said Dick, "it isn't. Tom's right. You've got everything that they have, and then some. Winters' rise ball is certainly a peach, but it hasn't the quick jump yours has just before it gets to the plate. My eye isn't so bad, but in practice I bat under it every time. Even when I don't miss it altogether, I hit it on the underside and raise a fly to the fielders. It's almost impossible to line it out. And your fast high one is so speedy that a fellow backs away from the plate when he sees it coming. I don't know that your outcurve is any better than Benson's, but you certainly have it under better control."

"On the dead quiet," he went on, "I'm rather worried about Winters this year, anyway. I think he's gone back. He's in with a fast bunch, and I fear has been going the pace. His fine work in the box last year made him a star and turned his head. It brought him a lot of popularity, and I'm afraid he isn't the kind that can stand prosperity. He doesn't go at his work in the right spirit this year. You all saw how he shirked the other day when we were training for wind."

They readily recalled the incident to which Dick alluded. The practice had been strenuous that day, but the coach had been insistent. As a wind up, he had called for a run around the track to perfect their wind and endurance, as well as to get off some of the superfluous flesh that still interfered with their development. The players were tired, but, as the trainer didn't ask them to do what he was unwilling to do himself, they lined up without protest and trotted behind him around the track.

At one place, there was a break in the fence which had not yet been repaired. Twice they made the circuit of the track, and some of them were blowing hard, when the relentless leader started on the third round. As they came abreast of the break, Winters, with a wink, slipped out of the line and got behind the fence. Here he stayed, resting, while the others jogged along. They made two circuits more, and when they came to where he was,

Winters, fresh as a daisy, and grinning broadly, slipped into line again, and trotted along as though nothing had happened. The joke seemed certainly on the coach, who hadn't once turned his head, but pounded steadily along, in apparent unconsciousness that one of his sheep had not been following his leader. At the bench, after the sixth round, he slowed up.

"Good work, boys," he said pleasantly, "that makes six full laps for all of us except Winters. We'll wait here, while he takes his other two."

The grin faded from Winters' face, to be replaced by a hot flush, as his eyes fell before the steady look of the coach. There was no help for it, however. He had been caught "red-handed," and with a sheepish glance at his laughing comrades, he started on his lonely run around the course while they stood and watched him. Twice he made the circuit and then rejoined his companions. The coach said nothing more, as he felt that the culprit had been punished enough, but the story was too good to keep, and Winters was "joshed" unmercifully by his mates. The incident deepened the general respect felt for the coach, and confirmed the conviction that it was useless to try to fool him, as he had "eyes in the back of his head."

He certainly needed all his keenness, in order to accomplish the task he had set himself. The time was wearing away rapidly, and before long he would have to rejoin his own team for the championship season. There had been a good deal of rain, and practice in the field had been impossible for days at a time.

To be sure he had the "cage" for use in rainy weather. This was a large rectangular enclosure, perhaps twice as long as the distance from the pitcher's box to home plate. The sides were made of rope that stopped the batted balls. There was ample room for battery work, and here, in bad weather, the pitchers and catchers toiled unceasingly, while the other players cultivated their batting eye, and kept their arms limber by tossing the ball about. But, at best, it was a makeshift, and did not compare for a moment with work in the open air on the actual diamond. And the days that now remained for that were distressingly few.

So he drove them on without mercy. No galley slaves worked harder than these college boys for their temporary master. He was bound that not an ounce of superfluous flesh should remain on their bones at the beginning of the season. Gradually his work began to tell. The soreness and lameness of the first days disappeared. Arnica and witch hazel were no longer at a premium. The waistbands went in and the chests stood out. Their eyes grew bright, their features bronzed, their muscles toughened, and before long they were like a string of greyhounds tugging at the leash.

He noted the change with satisfaction. Superb physical condition was the first essential of a winning team. His problem, however, was far from solved. It was only changed. He had made them athletes. Now he must make them ball players.

Individually they were that already, in the purely mechanical features of the game. They were quick fielders, speedy runners and heavy batters. But they might be all these, and yet not be a winning team. They needed team work, the deft fitting in of each part with every other, the quick thinking that, in a fraction of a second, might change defeat to victory.

His quick eye noticed, in the practice games, how far they came short of his ideal. Flynn, the other day, when he caught that fly far out in center, had hurled it into the plate when he had no earthly chance of getting the runner. If he had tried for Ames, who was legging it to third, it would have been an easy out. A moment later Ames counted on a single.

Then there was that bonehead play, when, with Hinsdale on third and Hodge on first, he had given the signal for Hodge to make a break for second, so as to draw a throw from the catcher and thus let Hinsdale get in from third. Hodge had done his part all right, but Hinsdale had been so slow in starting that the catcher was waiting for him with the ball, when he was still twenty feet from the plate.

He hated to think of that awful moment, when, with the bases full, White had deliberately tried to steal second, where Dick was already roosting. The crestfallen way in which White had come back to the bench, amid ironical cheers and boisterous laughter, was sufficient guarantee that that particular piece of foolishness would never be repeated. Luckily, it had only been in a practice game. Had it happened in a regular contest, a universal roar would have gone up from one end of the college world to the other, and poor White would never have heard the last of it.

The coach was still sore from this special exhibition of "solid ivory," when, after their bath and rubdown, he called the boys together.

"Now, fellows," he said, "I am going to talk to you as though you were human beings, and I want you to bring your feeble intelligence to bear, while I try to get inside your brain pans. They say that Providence watches over drunkards, fools and the Congress of the United States. I hope it also includes this bunch of alleged ball players. If ever any aggregation needed special oversight, this crowd of ping-pong players needs it. Now, you candidates for the old ladies' home, listen to me."

And listen they did, while he raked them fore and aft and rasped and scorched them, until, when he finally let them go, their faces were flaming. No one else in college could have talked to them that way and "gotten away with it." But his word was law, his rule absolute, and, behind his bitter tongue, they realized his passion for excellence, his fierce desire of winning. It was sharp medicine, but it acted like a tonic, and every man left the "dissecting room," as Tom called it, determined from that time on he would play with his brains as well as his muscles.

As the three chums went toward their rooms, they were overtaken by "Reddy," the trainer of the team. With the easy democracy of the ball field, he fell into step and joined in the conversation.

"Pretty hot stuff the old man gave you, just now," he said, with his eyes twinkling.

"Right you are," replied Bert, "but I guess we deserved it. I don't wonder that he was on edge. It certainly was some pretty raw baseball he saw played to-day."

"Sure," assented Reddy, frankly. "It almost went the limit. And yet," he went on consolingly, "it might have been worse. He only tried to steal one base with a man already on it. Suppose he'd tried to steal three."

The boys laughed. Reddy was a privileged character about the college. The shock of fiery hair, from which he had gained his nickname, covered a shrewd, if uneducated, mind. He had formerly been a big league star, but had fractured an ankle in sliding to second. The accident had only left a slight limp, but it had effectually destroyed his usefulness on the diamond. As a trainer and rubber, however, he was a wonder, and for many years he had been connected with the college in that capacity. It was up to him to keep the men in first-class condition, and he prided himself on his skill. No "charlie horse" could long withstand his ministrations, and for strains and sprains of every kind he was famous in the athletic world. His interest in and loyalty to the college was almost as great as that of the students themselves. He was in the full confidence of the coach, and was regarded by the latter as his right hand. If one was the captain of the college craft, the other was the first mate, and between them they made a strong combination. He was an encyclopedia of information on the national game. He knew the batting and fielding averages of all the stars for many years past, and his shrewd comments on men and things made him a most interesting companion. His knowledge of books might be limited, but his knowledge of the world was immense. He had taken quite a fancy to Bert and shared the conviction of the coach that he was going to be a tower of strength to the team. He never missed an opportunity of giving him pointers, and Bert had profited greatly by his advice and suggestion. Now, as they walked, he freed his mind along the same lines followed by the coach a little earlier.

"That was the right dope that Ainslee gave you, even if it was mixed with a little tabasco," he said. "It's the 'inside stuff' that counts. I'd rather have a team of quick thinkers than the heaviest sluggers in the league.

"Why," he went on, warming to his subject, "look at the Phillies when Ed Delehanty, the greatest natural hitter that ever lived, was in his prime. Say, I saw that fellow once make four home runs in one game against Terry of the Brooklyns. I don't suppose that a heavier batting bunch ever existed than the one they had in the league for three seasons, handrunning. Besides Ed himself, there was Flick and Lajoie, and a lot of others of the same kind, every one of them fence-breakers. You couldn't blame any pitcher for having palpitation of the heart when he faced that gang. They were no slouches in the field, either. Now, you'd naturally think that nobody would have a chance against them. Every year the papers touted them to win the pennant, but every year, just the same, they came in third or fourth at the end of the season. Now, why was it they didn't cop the flag? I'll tell you why. It was because every man was playing for himself. He was looking out for his record. Every time a man came to the bat, he'd try to lose the ball over the back fence. They wouldn't bunt, they wouldn't sacrifice, they wouldn't do anything that might hurt that precious record of theirs. It was every man for himself and no man for the team, and they didn't have a manager at the head of them that was wise enough or strong enough to make them do as they were told.

"Now, on the other hand, look at the White Sox. Dandy fielders, but for batting—why, if they fell in the river they wouldn't strike the water. All around the league circuit, they were dubbed the 'Hitless Wonders.' But they were quick as cats on their feet, and just as quick in knowing what to do at any stage of the game. What hits they did get counted double. They didn't get men on the bases as often as the Phillies, but they got them home oftener, and that's what counts when the score is added up. That sly old fox, Comiskey, didn't miss a point. It was a bunt or a sacrifice or a long fly to the outfield or waiting for a base on balls or anything else he wanted. The men forgot about themselves and only thought of the team, and thosesame 'Hitless Wonders' won the pennant in a walk.

"Now, that's just the difference between dumb and brainy playing and that's what makes Ainslee so hot when he sees a bonehead stunt like that one this afternoon."

"I suppose that you saw no end of that inside stuff pulled off while you were in the big league," said Tom. "What do you think is the brightest bit of thinking you ever saw on the ball field?"

"Well," said Reddy musingly, "that's hard to tell. I've certainly seen some stunts on the diamond that would make your hair curl. Some of them went through, and others were good enough to go through, even if they didn't. It often depends on the way the umpire looks at it. And very often it gets by, because the umpire doesn't look at it at all. Many's the time I've seen Mike Kelly of the old Chicagos — the receiving end of the ten-thousand-dollar battery — cut the corners at third when the umpire wasn't looking, and once I saw him come straight across the diamond from second to the plate without even making a bluff of going to third. Oh, he was a bird, was Mike.

"I shall never forget one day when the Chicagos were behind until they came to the plate for their ninth inning. They were a husky bunch of swatters and never more dangerous than when they were behind. Well, they made two runs in that inning, tieing the score and then putting themselves one to the good. The Bostons came in for their last turn at the bat and by the time two men were out they had the bases full. One safe hit to the outfield was all they needed, and they sent a pinch-hitter to the bat to bring in the fellows that were dancing about on the bases.

"It was a dreary, misty afternoon, and, from the grandstand you could hardly see the fielders. Mike was playing right that day, and the man at the bat sent a screaming liner out in his direction. He saw at a glance that he couldn't possibly get his hands on it, but he turned around and ran with the ball, and, at the last moment, jumped into the air and apparently collared it. He waved his hands as a signal that he had it and made off to the clubhouse. The umpire called the batter out and the game was over. His own teammates hadn't tumbled to the trick, until Mike told them that he hadn't come anywhere near the ball, and that at that very moment it was somewhere out on the playing field. It came out later, and there was some talk of protesting the game, but nothing ever came of it. When it came to quick work, Mike was certainly 'all wool and a yard wide.'"

The boys did not express an opinion as to the moral quality of the trick, and Reddy went on:

"Perhaps the slickest thing I ever saw was one that Connie Mack put over on old Cap Anson of the Chicagos, and, believe me, anybody who could fool him was going some. His playing days are over now, and all you kids know of him is by reputation, but, take him by and large, a better player never pulled on a glove. Well, as I was saying, Anson was playing one day in Pittsburgh and Mack was catching against him. It had been a game of hammer and tongs right up to the last inning. The Chicagos, as the visiting team, came to the bat first in the ninth inning. The Pittsburghs were one ahead and all they needed to win was to hold the Chicagos scoreless. Two were out and two on bases when old 'Pop' Anson came to the bat. There wasn't a man in the league at that time that a pitcher wouldn't rather have seen facing him than the 'Big Swede.' However, there was no help for it, and the twirler put on extra steam and managed to get two strikes on him. The old man set himself for the third, with fierce determination to 'kill' the ball or die in the attempt. Mack walked up to the pitcher and told him to send in a ball next time, and then, the instant the ball was returned to him, to put over a strike. The pitcher did as directed, and sent over a wide one. Of course, Anson didn't offer to hit it, but Mack caught it.

"'Third strike,' he said, throwing off his mask and shin-guards, as though the game were over.

"'Third strike nothing,' growled Anson. 'What's the matter with you, anyway?' and the umpire also motioned Connie back to the plate.

"'Why, wasn't that a strike?' said Mack, coming back to the plate. At the same instant the pitcher sent a beauty right over the center of the rubber.

Mack caught it, and before Anson knew the ball had been pitched, the umpire said, 'You're out.'

"Holler? Say, you could have heard him from Pittsburgh to Chicago. It went, though. You see, Anson, looking at Connie without his mask or shin-guards, was figuring that he would have to get into all that harness again, before the game went on. He took too much for granted, and it doesn't pay to do that in baseball. I don't suppose he ever forgave Connie for making him look like thirty cents before that holiday crowd. And I don't suppose that Mack would have taken a thousand dollars for the satisfaction it gave him to tally one on the old man.

"You fellows wouldn't believe me, I suppose, if I told you I seen a dog pull some of that inside stuff once? Sure, I ain't fooling, although of course the pup didn't know he was doing it. It was in Detroit when a big game was on and the home team was at the bat. They needed three runs to win and there were two men on bases. The batter lined out a peach between left and center. There were no automobiles in those days, but a whole raft of carriages were down back of center field. A big coach dog saw the ball coming and chased it, got it in his mouth and scooted down under the bleachers, the left and center fielders yelling to him to drop it and racing after him like mad. He was a good old rooter for the home team, all right, though, and, by the time they got it away from him, the whole bunch had crossed the plate and the game was won. The home team boys found out whom he belonged to, and clubbed together and got him a handsome collar.

"Another funny thing I seen one time that makes me laugh whenever I think of it," continued Reddy, "was when a high fly was hit to left field with three men on bases. It ought to have been an easy out and nine times out of ten would have been. But, as luck would have it, the ball slipped through the fielder's fingers and went into the outside upper pocket of his baseball shirt. He tried desperately to get it out, but it was wedged in so tight he couldn't. All this time the men were legging it around the bases. At last, Mitchell—that was the fellow's name—ran in toward third and caught the batter, just as he was rounding the base on his way to home. He grabbed him and hugged him tight and they fell to the ground together. Say, you'd have died laughing if you'd seen them two fellows wrestling, Mitchell trying to force the other man's hand into his pocket so that the ball could touch him, and the other fighting to keep his hand out. It was a hard thing for the umpire to settle, but he finally let the run count on the ground that Mitchell had no right to interfere with him. Poor old Mitchell was certainly up against it that day, good and plenty."

By this time they had reached the college dormitory, and the boys reluctantly bade Reddy good-by. They had been immensely amused and interested by his anecdotes, although they did not altogether agree with his easy philosophy of life. To Reddy all was fair in love or war or baseball, provided you could "put it over."

"But it isn't," said Bert, as they went upstairs. "Strategy is one thing and cheating is another. It's all right to take your opponent unawares and take advantage of his carelessness or oversight. If he's slow and you're quick, if he's asleep and you're awake, you've got a perfect right to profit by it. Now take for instance that case of Mack and Anson. Whether that was a strike or a ball was a thing to be decided by the umpire alone, and Anson ought not to have paid any attention to Mack's bluff. Then, too, because Mack usually put on his mask and shin-guards before the ball was pitched, Anson had no right to assume that he would always do so. Mack acted perfectly within his rights, and Anson was simply caught napping and had no kick coming.

"But when you come to 'cutting the corners' and pretending that the ball was caught when it wasn't, that isn't straight goods. It's 'slick,' all right, but it is the slickness of the crooked gambler and the three-card monte man. It's playing with marked cards and loaded dice, and I don't care for any of it in mine."

"Right you are, old fellow," said Tom, heartily, clapping him on the back, "my sentiments to a dot. I want to win and hate to lose, but I'd rather lose a game any day than lie or cheat about it."

Which he was to prove sooner than he expected.

CHAPTER IV

THE TRIPLE PLAY

The days flew rapidly by and the time drew near for the Spring trip. All the members of the team were to get a thorough trying out in actual games with the crack teams of various colleges before the regular pennant race began. Then the "weeding out" process would have been completed, and only those remain on the team who had stood the test satisfactorily. The trip was to take about two weeks, and they were to "swing around the circle" as far west as Cincinnati and as far south as Washington.

They did not expect much trouble in coming back with a clean score. As one of the "Big Three," their team was rarely taken into camp by any of the smaller colleges. They usually won, occasionally tied, but very seldom lost. Yet, once in a while, their "well-laid schemes" "went agley" and they met with a surprise party from some husky team that faced them unafraid and refused to be cowed by their reputation.

Bert's college was one of the largest and most important in the country. The "Big Three" formed a triangular league by themselves alone. Each played three games with each of the other two, and the winner of the majority was entitled to claim the championship of the "Big Three." And it was generally, though not officially, admitted, that the team capable of such a feat was the greatest college baseball team in the whole country. Their games were followed by the papers with the greatest interest and fully reported. The "Blues," as Bert's college was usually referred to on account of the college colors, had won the pennant the year before from the "Grays" and the "Maroons," their traditional opponents, after a heart-breaking struggle, and columns of newspaper space had been devoted to the concluding game. This year, however, the prediction had been freely made that history would not repeat itself. Both the Grays and Maroons were composed of tried and tested veterans, while, as we have seen, Ainslee had been compelled to fill several important positions with new material. No matter how good this might prove to be, it takes time and practice to weld it together in one smooth machine, and it is seldom done in a single season.

Moreover, the time was at hand when Ainslee would have to rejoin his own team, and his keen eye still noted a number of rough places thatneeded planing and polishing. For this reason he was all the more anxious to secure good results during this trip. After it was over, he would have to turn over the team to a manager and to Reddy, the assistant coach and trainer. The manager would confine himself chiefly to the technical and financial features, but it was arranged that Reddy should have full charge of the team on the field. Ainslee reposed implicit confidence in him because of his shrewd judgment, his knowledge of men, and his vast baseball experience.

West Point was to be their first stop, and it was a jolly crowd, full of the joy and zest of living, that embarked on the steamer Hendrik Hudson, and sailed up the lordly river, the finest in the world, as most of the boys agreed, though some, who had traveled, were inclined to favor the claims of the Rhine to that distinction. They were disposed to envy the Dutch explorer, who, first among civilized men, had sailed up the river that bore his name and feasted his eyes upon its incomparable beauty; a delight that contrasted so strongly with the final scene when he and his little son had been thrust by a mutinous crew into an open boat on storm-tossed Arctic waters, and left to perish miserably. The reward, as Dick cynically insisted, of most of the world's great benefactors, who have been stoned, burned, or otherwise slain by their fellows, while posterity, too late, has crowned them with laurels and honored them with monuments.

The game with Uncle Sam's cadets was a fight "for blood," as was entirely appropriate for future soldiers. In the seventh, with the cadets one run behind, one of them attempted to steal from second to third. Hinsdale got the ball down to Tom like a shot, but, in the mix-up, it was hard to tell whether the runner had made the base or not. The umpire at first called it out, but the captain of the cadets kicked so vigorously that the umpire asked Tom directly whether he had touched him in time.

For an instant Tom hesitated, but only for an instant. Then he straightened up and answered frankly:

"No, I didn't; he just beat me to it."

It is only just to Tom's companions to say that, after the first minute of disappointment, they felt that he could and should have done nothing else. The standard of college honor is high, and when it came to a direct issue, few, if any, of the boys would have acted differently. Even Reddy, with his free and easy views on winning games "by hook or crook," as long as you win them, felt a heightened respect for Tom, although he shook his head dubiously when the man from third came home on a sacrifice, tieing the score.

The tie still persisted in the ninth, and the game went into extra innings. In the tenth the Blues scored a run and the cadets made a gallant effort to do the same, or even "go them one better." A man was on second and another on third, when one of their huskiest batters came to the plate. He caught the ball squarely "on the seam" and sent it straight toward third, about two feet over Tom's head. He made a tremendous jump, reached up his gloved hand and the ball stuck there. That of course put out the batter. The man on third, thinking it was a sure hit, was racing to the plate. As Tom came down, he landed right on the bag, thus putting out the runner, who had turned and was desperately trying to get back. In the meantime the man on second, who had taken a big lead, had neared third. As he turned to go back to second, Tom chased him and touched him just before he reached the bag. Three men were out, the game was won, and Tom was generously cheered, even by the enemy, while his comrades went wild. He had made a "triple play unassisted," the dream of every player and one of the rarest feats ever "pulled off" on the baseball diamond.

During the trip, Winters and Benson occupied the pitcher's box more often than Bert, and it was evident that, despite Bert's showing in the early spring practice, both Ainslee and Reddy were more inclined to pin their faith this season on their tested stars than on the new recruit. They really believed that Bert had "more on the ball" than either of the others, but were inclined to let him have a year on the bench before putting him in for the "big" games. They knew the tremendous importance of experience and they also knew how nerve-racking was the strain of playing before a crowd of perhaps twenty-five thousand frenzied rooters. Bert might do this, but Winters and Benson had actually done it, and they could not leave this significant fact out of their calculations. So they carried him along gradually, never letting up on their instruction and advice and occasionally putting him in to pitch one or two innings to relieve the older men after the game was pretty surely won.

Bert was too sensible and sportsmanlike to resent this, and followed with care and enthusiasm the training of his mentors. A better pair of teachers could not have been found and Bert made rapid progress. Something new was constantly coming up, and, as he confided to Dick, he never dreamed there was such a variety of curves. There was "the hook," "the knuckle," "the palm," "the high floater," "the thumb jump," "the cross fire," and so many others that there seemed to be no end to them. But though he sought to add them all to his repertory, he followed Ainslee's earnest urging to perfect his wonderful fadeaway, and gave more attention to that than to any other.

"And to think," he said to Tom, one day, "it isn't so very long ago that people didn't believe it was possible to throw a curve ball at all and learned men wrote articles to show that it couldn't be done."

"Yes," said Tom, "they remind me of the eminent scientist who wrote a book proving, to his own satisfaction, at least, that a vessel couldn't cross the Atlantic under steam. But the first copy of the book that reached America was brought over by a steamer."

"Yes," chimed in Dick, "they were like the farmer who had read the description of a giraffe and thought it a fairy story. One day a circus came to town with a giraffe as one of its attractions. The farmer walked all around it, and then, turning to his friends, said stubbornly, 'There ain't no such animal.'"

Reddy joined in the laugh that followed and took up the conversation. "Well," he said, while the others in the Pullman car in which they were traveling drew around him, for they always liked to see him get started on his recollections, "the honor of having discovered the curve rests between Arthur Cummings and Bobby Mathews. It's never been clearly settled which 'saw it first.' Before their time it used to be straight, fast ones and a slow teaser that was thrown underhand. But even at that, don't run away with the idea that those old fellows weren't some pitchers. Of course, they were handicapped by the fact that at first they had to keep on pitching until the player hit it. The four-ball rule, and making a foul count for a hit, and all those modern things that have been invented to help the pitcher, hadn't been thought of then. Naturally, that made heavy batting games. Why, I know that the old Niagara team of Buffalo won a game once by 201 to 11."

"Yes," broke in Ainslee, "and the first college game in 1859 was won by Amherst over Williams by a score of 66 to 32."

"Gee," said Hinsdale, "the outfielders in those days must have had something to do, chasing the ball."

"They certainly did," agreed Reddy, "but, of course, that sort of thing didn't last very long. The pitchers soon got the upper hand, and then, good-by to the big scores.

"I suppose," he went on, "that the real beginning of baseball, as we know it to-day, goes back to the old 'Red Stockings' of Cincinnati, in '69 and '70. There was a team for you. George and Harry Wright and Barnes and Spalding, and a lot of others just as good, went over the country like a prairie fire. There wasn't anybody that could stand up against them. Why, they went all though one season without a single defeat. It got to be after a while that the other teams felt about them just as they say boxers used to feel when they stood up against Sullivan. They were whipped before they put up their hands. The next year they got their first defeat at the hands of the old Atlantics of Brooklyn. I was a wee bit of a youngster then, but I saw that game through a hole in the fence. Talk about excitement! At the end of the ninth inning the score was tied, and the Atlantics were anxious to stop right there. It was glory enough to tie the mighty Red Stockings—a thing that had never been done before—without taking any further chances. But Harry Wright, the captain, was stubborn—I guess he was sorry enough for it afterwards—and the game went on, only to have the Atlantics win in the eleventh by a score of 7 to 6. I've seen many a game since, but never one to equal that.

"Of course the game has kept on improving all the time. I ain't denying that. There used to be a good deal of 'rough stuff' in the old days. The gamblers started in to spoil it, and sometimes as much as $20,000 would be in the mutual pools that used to be their way of betting. Then, too, the players didn't use to get much pay and, with so much money up, it was a big temptation to 'throw' games. It got to be so, after a while, that you wouldn't know whether the game was on the level or not. The only salvation of the game was to have some good strong men organize and put it on a solid footing and weed out the grafters. They did this and got a gang of them 'dead to rights' in the old Louisville team. They expelled four of them and barred them from the game forever, and, although they moved heaven and earth to get back, they never did. And since that time the game has been as clean as a hound's tooth. As a matter of fact, it's about the only game in America, except perhaps football, that you can count on as being absolutely on the square.

"It's a great sport, all right, and I don't wonder it is called the national game. It's splendid exercise for every muscle of the body and every faculty of the brain. Rich or poor, great or small, everybody with a drop of sporting blood in his veins likes it, even if he can't play it. At the Washington grounds a box seat is reserved for the President, and I notice that no matter how heavy the 'cares of state,' he's usually on hand and rooting for the home team. Why, I've heard that when the committee went to notify Lincoln that he was nominated for President, he was out at the ball ground, playing 'one old cat,' and the committee had to wait until he'd had his turn at bat. It may not be true, but it's good enough to be."

"And not only is it our national game," put in Ainslee, "but other countries are taking it up as well. They have dandy baseball teams in Cuba and Japan, that would make our crack nines hustle to beat them, and, in Canada, it is already more popular than cricket."

"I've heard," said Tom, "that not long ago they made a cable connection with some island way up in the Arctic Circle. The World's Series was being played then, and the very first message that came over the cable from the little bunch of Americans up there was: 'What's the score?'"

"Yes," laughed Ainslee, "it gets in the blood, and with the real 'dyed in the wool' fan it's the most important thing in the world. You've heard perhaps of the pitcher who was so dangerously sick that he wasn't expected to live. The family doctor stood at the bedside and took his temperature. He shook his head gravely.

"'It's 104,' he said.

"'You're a liar,' said the pitcher, rousing himself, 'my average last season was .232, and it would have been more if the umpire hadn't robbed me.'"

The train drew up at Washington just then, and the laughing crowd hustled to get their traps together. Here they played the last game of the season with the strong Georgetown University nine, and just "nosed them out" in an exciting game that went eleven innings. While in the city they visited the Washington Monument, that matchless shaft of stone that dwarfs everything else in the National Capital. Of course the boys wanted to try to catch a ball dropped from the top, but the coach would not consent.

"Only two or three men in the world have been able to do that," he said, "and they took big chances. I've had too much trouble getting you fellows in good condition, to take any needless risks."

So the boys turned homeward, bronzed, trained, exultant over their string of well-earned victories, and, in the approving phrase of Reddy, "fit to fight for a man's life." Ainslee left them at New York to join his team amid a chorus of cheers from the young athletes that he had done so much to form. From now on, it was "up to them" to justify his hopes and bring one more pennant to the dear old Alma Mater.

CHAPTER V

WINNING HIS SPURS

"Play ball!" shouted the umpire, and the buzz of conversation in the grandstand ceased. All eyes were fastened on the two teams about to enter on the first important game of the season, and people sat up straight and forgot everything else, so great was their interest in the forthcoming event.

All the games that the Blues had played up to this time had been with teams over which they felt reasonably sure of winning a victory, but the nine they had to face to-day was a very different proposition. Most of the young fellows composing it were older and had had more experience than the Blues, and the latter knew that they would have to do their very utmost to win, if win they did. The thing they most relied on, however, was the fact that their pitcher was very good, and they believed that he would probably win the day for them.

Of course, they had a lot of confidence in themselves, too, but the importance of a steady, efficient pitcher to any team can hardly be exaggerated. It gives them a solid foundation on which to build up a fast, winning team, and nobody realized this better than Mr. Ainslee, their veteran coach.

"Only give me one good pitcher," he was wont to say, "and I'll guarantee to turn out a team that will win the college championship."

The star on the college team this year, Winters, was, without doubt, an exceptionally good pitcher. He had considerable speed and control, and his curves could generally be counted on to elude the opposing batsmen. He was the only son in a wealthy family, however, and, as a consequence, had a very exaggerated idea of his own importance. He was inclined to look down on the fellows who did not travel in what he called "his set," and often went out of his way to make himself disagreeable to them.

As Dick put it, "He liked to be the 'main squeeze,'" and he had been much irritated over the way in which Bert had attracted the coach's attention, and the consequent talk on the campus regarding the "new pitcher." He and his friends made it a point to sneer at and discredit these stories, however, and to disparage Bert on every possible occasion.

The veteran trainer had not forgotten, however, and moreover he was worried in secret about Winters. It was, of course, his duty to see that all the players attended strictly to business, and let no outside interests interfere with their training. Of late, however, he had heard from several sources that Winters had been seen in the town resorts at various times when he was supposed to be in bed, and Reddy knew, none better, what that meant.

However, he hoped that the pitcher would not force him to an open rebuke, and so had said nothing as yet. Nevertheless, as has been said, he kept Bert in mind as a possible alternative, although he hoped that he would not be forced to use him.

"He's had too little experience yet," he mused. "If I should put him in a game, he'd go up like a rocket, most likely. Them green pitchers can't be relied upon, even if he did fool Ainslee," and the veteran, in spite of his worry, was forced to smile over the memory of how Bert had struck the great coach out in practice.

Previous to the actual start of the game both teams had been warming up on the field, and each had won murmurs of applause from the grandstands. To the wise ones, however, it was apparent that the Blues were a trifle shaky in fielding work, and many were seen to shake their heads dubiously.

"The youngsters will have to do some tall hustling if they expect to win from the visitors," one gray-haired man was heard to say, "but they say they have a crackerjack pitcher, that's one thing in their favor."

"Yes, of course," agreed his friend, "but it's not only that; the other fellows have had a whole lot more experience than our boys. And that counts an awful lot when it comes to a pinch."

"You're right, it does," acquiesced the other; "however, there's no use crossing the bridge till we come to it. We'll hope for the best, anyway."

After a little more practice both teams retired to the clubhouse to make their last preparations. Not many minutes later everything was in readiness, and the teams trotted into their positions. Of course, the visitors went to bat first, and then could be heard the umpire's raucous cry of "Play ball!" that ushered in the game.

A wave of handclapping and a storm of encouraging shouts and yells swept over the grandstand, and then ensued a breathless silence. The first two balls Winters pitched were wild, but then he steadied down, and struck the first batter out. The second man up swung wildly, but after having two strikes called, popped an easy fly toward first base that Dick smothered "easier than rolling off a log," as he afterwards said. The third man met with no better fate, and Winters struck him out with apparent ease.

As the fielders trotted in, the elderly gentleman who had entertained such doubts before chuckled, "Well, now if our boys can only get in a little stick work, and keep on holding them down like this, it looks as though they might win, after all."

Tom was the first man up at the bat for the Blues. But the pitcher opposed to him had lots of "stuff" on his delivery, and the best Tom could do was to lift an easy foul that dropped into the catcher's glove.

The next man up was struck out, as was also the third, and the inning ended without a run for either team.

From his seat on the substitutes' bench, Bert had watched the game up to this point with eager eyes, and had felt that he would almost have given ten years of his life to take part in it. He knew there was practically no chance of this, however, and so with a sigh of regret settled back to watch the further progress of the game.

The next two innings also passed without a run scored on either side, and it became more and more evident as the game went on that this was to be a pitchers' battle.

The first man up at bat for the visitors at the beginning of the fourth inning was considered their heaviest hitter, and as he walked up to the plate he was swinging two bats, one of which he threw aside as he stepped to the plate. From the way he crouched in readiness for the ball it could be seen that he meant business, and the coach called Winters over to him.

"You want to be mighty careful what you feed this man," he whispered, "and whatever you do, keep them low. He likes high balls, and if you give him one up as high as his shoulder, he'll swat it, sure."

"Oh, you can bet he won't get a hit off me," replied Winters, carelessly. "I've got that team eating out of my hand."

"Don't be too sure of that, my lad," warned the coach, but Winters only smiled in a superior fashion and strolled back to the box.

The first ball he pitched was an incurve, but it looked good to the batter, and he swung at it viciously. He missed it clean, and the umpire shouted, "One strike!"

This made Winters a little careless, and the next ball he pitched was just the one that the coach had warned him against. The batter took a step forward, swung fiercely at the ball, and there was a sharp crack as the ball and bat connected. The ball shot back with the speed of a bullet, and the outfielders started in hopeless chase. Baird, the batter, tore around the bases, and amid a veritable riot of cheering from the visiting rooters and a glum silence from the home supporters, charged across the sack for a home run!

Too late now Winters thought of Reddy's warning, and wished he had given it more heed. He knew that in so close a contest as this promised to be, one run would probably be enough to win the game, and this knowledge made him nervous. The breaks from training that he had been guilty of lately began to tell, also, and he commenced to lose confidence, a fatal thing in a pitcher. However, he managed to get through the inning somehow, and walked to the bench with a crestfallen air.

The coach forbore to reproach him just then, as he knew that it would probably do more harm than good. However, he kept a sharp eye on him, and inwardly was very much worried. He knew that Benson was not speedy enough to stand much chance against as strong a team as they were now playing, and though a great admirer of Bert, he did not know whether he had the stamina to go a full game. He resolved to give Winters every chance to recover himself, and prayed that he would be able to do so.

The first man of the home team to go to bat struck out on the hot curves served up to him, but Dick connected with the ball for a clean two-base hit. A great cheer went up at this feat, but it was destined to have little effect. The second man fouled out and the third raised an easy fly to the pitcher's box, and so Dick's pretty drive did them no good.

In the fifth inning Winters' pitching became more and more erratic, and to Reddy's experienced eye it became evident that he would soon "blow up." So he strolled over to the substitutes' bench and sat down beside Bert.

"How does your arm feel to-day, Wilson?" he inquired. "Do you feel as though you could pitch if I happened to need you?"

Bert's heart gave a great leap, but he managed to subdue his joy as he realized the trainer's meaning, and answered, "Why, yes, I think I could make out all right. Do you think you will need me?"

"Well, there's just a chance that I may," replied Reddy, "and I want you to be ready to jump out and warm up the minute I give you the signal."

"I'll be ready, sir, I can promise you that," replied Bert, earnestly, and the trainer appeared a little more hopeful as he turned away.

"I can at least count on that young chap doing the best that is in him, at any rate," he thought; "he certainly doesn't look like a quitter to me."

In their half of the fifth inning the home team was unable to make any headway against the opposing pitcher's curves, which seemed to get betterand better as the game progressed. Dick felt, in some mysterious way, that his team was losing heart, and his one hope was that the coach would give Bert a chance to pitch. The boys, one after another, struck out or lifted easy flies, and not one man reached first base.

The visitors now came to bat again, and the first ball Winters pitched was slammed out into left field for a two-base hit. The next batter up stepped to the plate with a grin on his face, and one of his teammates called, "Go to it, Bill. Eat 'em alive. We've got their goat now."

The man thus adjured leaned back, and as Winters delivered a slow, easy ball he swung viciously and sent a smoking grounder straight for the pitcher's box. The ball passed Winters before he had time to stoop for it, but White, the shortstop, made a pretty pick-up, and slammed the ball to Dick at first. The ball arrived a second too late to put the runner out, however, and in the meantime the first man had reached third. Now was a crucial moment, and everything depended on the pitcher. All eyes were fastened on him, but from something in his attitude Reddy knew that he was on the verge of a breakdown. Nor was he mistaken in this, for out of the next five balls Winters pitched, only one strike was called. The rest were balls, and the umpire motioned to the batter to take first base. Of course this advanced the man on first to second base, thus leaving all the bases full and none out.

As Winters was winding up preparatory to delivering one of his erstwhile famous drops, Reddy motioned to Bert, and in a second the latter was up and had shed his sweater. He trotted over to where Reddy was standing, and said, "You wanted me, didn't you?"

"Yes," replied Reddy, in a tense voice; "get Armstrong there" — motioning toward the substitute catcher — "and warm up as quickly as you can. Take it easy, though!" he commanded; "don't start in too hard! You might throw your arm out on the first few balls. Just limber up gradually."

"All right, sir," replied Bert, and called to Armstrong.

In the meantime Winters had pitched two wild balls, and the visiting rooters were yelling like maniacs. The third ball was an easy inshoot, and the batter, making a nice calculation, landed it fair and square. It flew over into left field, between the pitcher's box and third base, and before it could be returned to the waiting catcher two runners had crossed the plate. This made the score three to none in favor of the visitors, with two men on base and none out. Matters looked hopeless indeed for the home team, and one of the spectators groaned, "It's all over now but the shouting, fellows. Winters is up higher than a kite, and we've got nobody to put in his place. This game will just be a slaughter from now on."

"How about young Wilson?" asked his friend. "I heard the other day that he had showed up pretty well in practice. It looks now as though Reddy meant to put him in the box. See, he's warming up over there right now."

"Ye gods and little fishes!" lamented the other. "Now we are cooked, for fair. It was bad enough with Winters pitching, but now when they put that greenhorn Freshie in, we'll just be a laughing stock, that's all. Why doesn't the band play the funeral march?"

"Aw, wait and see," said the other. "I don't suppose we've got the ghost of a show, but Dick Trent was telling me of some pretty good stunts this boy Wilson has pulled off before this. He was telling me about a race in which Wilson drove a car across the tape a winner after a dickens of a grilling race. Any fellow that's got nerve enough to drive a racing auto ought to be able to hold his own at baseball or anything else. You just sit tight and don't groan so much, and he may show us something yet."

"Forget it, Bill, forget it," returned the other. "They've got our team running, and they'll keep it running, take my word for it."

"That's right," agreed another, "we might as well go home now as to wait for the slaughter. This game is over, right now."

"Hey, look at that!" yelled the first speaker, excitedly. "There goes Wilson into the box. Three cheers for Wilson, fellows. Now! One! two! three!"

The cheers were given by the faithful fans, but they had given up hope. It was indeed, as the rooter had said, however, and Bert was actually being given an opportunity to pitch in a big game, when he had only been with the team a few months! Many a pitcher has been a substitute until his junior year, and never had a chance like this one. And, to tell the truth, Reddy himself would have been the last one to put what he considered an inexperienced pitcher into the box, if he had had any alternative. Now, however, it was a case of having no choice, because he knew that the game was irretrievably lost if Winters continued to pitch, so he put Bert in as a forlorn hope, but without any real expectation that he would win.

As he noticed the confident way in which Bert walked to the box, however, he plucked up courage a little, but immediately afterward shook his head. "Pshaw," he thought, "they've got too big a lead on us. If Wilson can only hold them down so that they don't make monkeys of us, it will be more than I have a right to hope."

For all Bert's nonchalant air, however, it must not be thought that he was not excited or nervous. He had had comparatively little baseball experience in such fast company as this. He had learned, however, to keep a cool and level head in times of stress, and he knew that everything depended on this. So he just gritted his teeth, and when he motioned to the catcher to come up and arrange signals, the latter hardly suspected what a turmoil was going on under Bert's cool exterior.

"Just take it easy, kid," he advised. "Don't try to put too much stuff on the ball at first, and pitch as though we were only practising back of the clubhouse. Don't let those blamed rooters get you nervous, either. Take your time before each ball, and we'll pull through all right. Now, just get out there, and show them what you've got."

Bert took his position in the box, and the umpire tossed him a brand new ball. Remembering the catcher's advice, he wound up very deliberately, and pitched a swift, straight one square over the middle of the plate. The batsman had expected the "greenhorn" to try a fancy curve, and so was not prepared for a ball of this kind. "One str-r-rike!" yelled the umpire, and the catcher muttered approvingly to himself. The batter, however, took a fresh grip on his bat, and resolved to "knock the cover off" the next one. Bert delivered a wide out curve, and the batter swung hard, but only touched the ball, for a foul, and had another strike called on him. "Aw, that kid's running in luck," he thought. "But watch me get to him this time."

The next ball Bert pitched looked like an easy one, and the batter, measuring its flight carefully with his eye, drew his bat back and swung with all the weight of his body. Instead of sending the ball over the fence, however, as he had confidently expected, the momentum of his swing was spent against empty air, and so great was its force that the bat flew out of his hand. "Three strikes," called the umpire, and amid a riot of cheering from the home rooters the batter gazed stupidly about him.

"By the great horn spoon," he muttered, under his breath, "somebody must have come along and stolen that ball just as I was going to hit it. I'll swear that if it was in the air when I swung at it that I would have landed it."

As he walked to the bench the captain said, "What's the matter with you, Al? Has the freshie got you buffaloed?"

"Aw, nix on that, cap," replied the disgruntled batter. "Wait until you get up there. Either that kid's having a streak of luck or else he's got that ball hypnotized. That last one he pitched just saw my bat coming and dodged under it. I think he's got 'em trained."

"Why, you poor simp," laughed the captain; "just wait till I get up there. Why, we all saw that last ball you bit on so nicely. It was a cinch, wasn't it, boys?"

It sure was, they all agreed, but the unfortunate object of these pleasantries shook his head in a puzzled way, and stared at Bert.

As it happened, the next batter was the same who had scored the home run in the first part of the game, and he swaggered confidently to the plate.

Bert had overheard what the coach had told Winters in regard to this batter, so he delivered a low ball, which the batter let pass. "One ball," called the umpire, and the captain of the visitors' team remarked, "I thought he couldn't last. That was just a streak of 'beginner's luck,' that's all."

The next ball looked good to the batsman, and he lunged hard at the white sphere. It was a tantalizing upshoot, however, and he raised an easy fly to Dick at first. The man on second had become so absorbed in watching Bert, that when Dick wheeled like lightning and snapped the ball to second, he was almost caught napping, and barely got back in time.

The home rooters, who up to now had been rather listless in their cheering, now started in with a rush, and a veritable storm of cheering and singing shook the grandstand. The coach drew a deep breath, and began to allow himself the luxury of a little hope.

The third man up was the captain, who had boasted so of what he was going to do to the "green" pitcher. As he rose to go to the plate he remarked, "Watch me, now, Al, and I'll show you what it is like to swat a ball over the fence."

He selected a very heavy bat, and stepped jauntily to the plate. Bert had been warned to do his best against this man, as he was popularly known as the "pitcher's hoodoo." He resolved to use his "fadeaway" ball for all it was worth, and shook his head at all the catcher's signals until the latter signaled for the fadeaway. He then nodded his head, and wound up very deliberately. Then he pitched what looked like a straight, fast ball to the expectant batsman. The latter gripped his bat and put all his strength into what he fondly hoped would be a "homer." His bat whistled as it cut the air, but in some mysterious way failed to even touch the ball, which landed with a loud "plunk!" in the catcher's mitt. A roar of derisive laughter went up from the rooters, and the captain looked rather foolish. "That's mighty queer," he thought, "there must be something the matter with the balance of this bat. I guess I'll try another." Accordingly, he took a fresh bat, and waited with renewed confidence for the next ball. This time he swung more carefully, but with no better result. "Two strikes!" barked the umpire, and the frenzied rooters stood up on their seats and yelled themselves hoarse. "Wilson! Wilson! Wilson!" they roared in unison, and Bert felt a great surge of joy go through him. His arm felt in perfect condition, and he knew that if called upon he could have pitched the whole game and not have been overtired. He handled the ball carefully, and fitted it in just the right position in his hand. He resolved to try the same ball once more, as he thought the batter would probably think that he would try something else. This he did, and although the batter felt sure that he had this ball measured to the fraction of an inch, his vicious swing encountered nothing more substantial than air.

"Three strikes!" called the umpire, and amid a storm of cheering and ridicule from the grandstand the discomfited batter slammed his bat down and walked over to his teammates.

It was now Al's turn to crow, and he did so unmercifully. "What's the matter, cap?" he inquired, grinning wickedly. "That kid hasn't got your goat, has he? Where's that homer over the fence that you were alluding to a few minutes ago?"

"Aw, shut up!" returned the captain, angrily. "That Freshie's got a delivery that would fool Ty Cobb. There's no luck about that. It's just dandy pitching."

"I could have told you that," said the other, "but I thought I'd let you find it out for yourself. That boy's a wonder."

The home team trotted in from the field eagerly, and there was a look in their eyes that Reddy was glad to see. "They've got some spirit and confidence in them now," he thought. "I certainly think I've got a kingpin pitcher at last. But I'd better not count my chickens before they're hatched. He may go all to pieces in the next inning."

As they came in, Dick and Tom slapped Bert on the back. "We knew you could do it, old scout!" they exulted. "What will old Winters' pals have to say after this?"

Reddy said little, but scanned Bert's face carefully, and seemed satisfied. "I guess you'll do, Wilson," he said. "We'll let you pitch this game out, and see what you can do."

Sterling was the first man up, and he walked to the plate with a resolve to do or die written on his face. He planted his feet wide apart, and connected with the first pitched ball for a hot grounder that got him safely to first base. The rooters cheered frantically, and the cheering grew when it was seen that Bert was the next batter. This was more in recognition, however, of his good work in the box. Heavy hitting is not expected of a pitcher, and nobody looked to see Bert do much in this line. While he had been watching the game from the bench, he had studied the opposing pitcher's delivery carefully, and had learned one or two facts regarding it. He felt sure that if the pitcher delivered a certain ball, he would be able to connect with it, but was disappointed at first. Bert bit at a wide out curve, and fouled the next ball, which was a fast, straight one. But as the pitcher wound up for the third one Bert's heart leaped, for he saw that this was going to be the ball that he had been hoping for. He grasped his bat near the end, for Bert was what is known as a "free swinger," and crouched expectantly. The ball came to him like a shot, but he swung his bat savagely and clipped the ball with terrific force toward third base. Almost before the spectators realized that the ball had been hit, Bert was racing toward first base, and the man already on base was tearing up the sod toward second.

The ball scorched right through the hands of the third baseman, and crashed against the left field fence. The fielders scurried wildly after it, but before they could return it to the infield, the man on first base had scored, and Bert was on third.

"We'll win yet! We'll win yet! We'll win yet!" croaked a rooter, too hoarse to yell any longer. "What's the matter with Wilson?" and in one vast roar came the answer, "HE'S ALL RIGHT!"

The home team players were all dancing around excitedly, and they pounded Hinsdale unmercifully on the back, for he was up next. "Bust a hole through the fence, Hinsdale," they roared; "they're on the run now. Go in and break a bat over the next ball!"

"Hin" fairly ran to the plate in his eagerness, and, as he afterward said, he felt as though he "couldn't miss if he tried." The first ball over the plate he slammed viciously at the pitcher, who stopped the ball, but fumbled it a few seconds, thus giving him a chance to get to first. The pitcher then hurled the ball to the home plate, in the hope of cutting off Bert from scoring, but was a fraction of a second too late, and Bert raced in with one more run.

The pitcher now tightened up, however, and put his whole soul into stopping this winning streak, and it looked as though he had succeeded. The next two batters struck out on six pitched balls, and the visiting rooters had a chance to exercise their voices, which had had a rest for some time. Drake was up next, and he knocked out a long fly that looked good, but was pulled down by a fielder after a pretty run. This ended the sixth inning, and the visitors were still one run ahead.

As Bert was about to go onto the field, Reddy said, "Don't take it too hard, Wilson. Don't mind if they do hit a ball sometimes. If you try to strike each man out without fail, it makes too great a tax on your arm. Let the fielders work once in a while."

With these instructions in mind, Bert eased up a little in the next inning, but the visitors had no chance to do any effective slugging. Twice they got a man on first base, but each time Bert struck out the following batter or only allowed him to hit the ball for an easy fly that was smothered without any trouble.

Consequently the visitors failed to score that inning, but they were still one run ahead, and knew that if they could hold Bert's team down they would win the game.

The home team failed to "get to" the ball for anything that looked like a run, and the seventh inning ended with no change in the score.

"Well, Wilson, it's up to you to hold them down," said Reddy, as the players started for their positions in the beginning of the eighth inning. "Do you feel as though you could do it?"

"Why, I'll do my best," replied Bert, modestly. "My arm feels stronger than it did when I started, so I guess I'm good for some time yet, at any rate."

"All right, go in and win," replied Reddy, with a smile, and Bert needed no urging.

The first man to bat for the visitors was the one called Al, who had first had a taste of Bert's "fadeaway." He swung viciously on the first ball that Bert offered him, which happened to be a fast in-curve. By a combination of luck and skill he managed to land the sphere for a safe trip to first. The cover of the ball was found to be torn when it was thrown back. Consequently, Bert had to pitch with a new ball, and failed to get his customary control. Much to his disgust he pitched four balls and two strikes, and the batter walked to first, forcing the man already on first to second base.

"Yah, yah!" yelled a visiting rooter. "It's all over. He's blowing up! Pitcher's got a glass arm! Yah! Yah!"

Others joined him in this cry, and Reddy looked worried. "That's enough to rattle any green pitcher," he thought. "I only hope they don't know what they're talking about, and I don't think they do. Wilson's a game boy, or I'm very much mistaken."

"Don't let 'em scare you, Bert," called Dick, from first base. "Let 'em yell their heads off if they want to. Don't mind 'em."

"No danger of that," returned Bert, confidently. "Just watch my smoke for a few minutes, that's all."

Bert struck out the next batter in three pitched balls, and the clamor from the hostile rooters died down. The next batter was the captain, and he was burning for revenge, but popped a high foul to Hinsdale, the catcher, and retired, saying things not to be approved. The third man was struck out after Bert had had two balls called on him, and this ended the visitors' half of the eighth inning.

The home team could make no better headway against the visitors' pitching and team work, however, and the inning ended without a tally. The score stood three to two in the visitors' favor, and things looked rather dark for the home boys.

At the beginning of the ninth the visitors sent a pinch hitter, named Burroughs, to the plate to bat in place of Al, who by now had an almost superstitious fear of Bert's delivery, and declared that "he couldn't hit anything smaller than a football if that Freshie pitched it."

Burroughs was hampered by no such feelings, however, and, after two strikes had been called on him, he managed to connect with a fast, straight ball and sent it soaring into the outfield. It looked like an easy out, but at the last moment the fielder shifted his position a little too much, and the ball dropped through his fingers. Before he could get it in, the runner had reached third base, where he danced excitedly and emitted whoops of joy.

Bert felt a sinking sensation at his heart, as he realized how much depended on him. The next man up made a clever bunt, and although he was put out, Burroughs reached home ahead of the ball, bringing in another run.

He was rewarded with a storm of applause from the visiting rooters, and it seemed as though all hope had departed for the home team.

With the next batter Bert made unsparing use of his fadeaway, and struck him out with little trouble. The third man shared the same fate, but it seemed as though the game were irretrievably lost. A two-run lead in the ninth inning seemed insurmountable, and Reddy muttered things under his breath. When the boys came trooping over to the bench, he said, "What's the matter with you fellows, anyway? What good does it do for Wilson to hold the other team down, if you don't do any stick work to back him up? Get in there now, and see if you can't knock out a few runs. A game is never finished until the last half of the ninth inning, and you've got a good chance yet. Go to it."

Every chap on the team resolved to make a run or die in the attempt, and Reddy could see that his speech had had some effect.

Dick was the first batter up, and he selected a heavy "wagon tongue" and stepped to the plate. The pitcher may have been a little careless, but at any rate Dick got a ball just where he wanted it, and swung with all his strength. The ball fairly whistled as it left the bat and dashed along the ground just inside the right foul line. Dick sprinted frantically around the bases, and got to third before he was stopped by Tom, who had been waiting for him. "No further, old sock," said Tom, excitedly. "That was a crackerjack hit, but you could never have got home on it. Gee! if Hodge will only follow this up we've got a chance."

Hodge was a good batter, and he waited stolidly until he got a ball that suited him. Two strikes were called on him, and still he waited. Then the pitcher sent him a long out curve, and Hodge connected with the ball for a safe one-bag hit, while Dick raced home. It looked bright for the home team now, but the next batter struck out, and although Hodge made a daring slide to second, a splendid throw cut him off.

Sterling was up next, and on the third pitched ball he managed to plant a short drive in left field that got him safely to first base. Then it was Bert's turn at the bat, and a great roar greeted him as he stepped to the plate.

"Win your own game, Wilson," someone shouted, and Bert resolved to do so, if possible.

He tried to figure out what the pitcher would be likely to offer him, and decided that he would probably serve up a swift, straight one at first. He set himself for this, but the pitcher had different ideas, and sent over a slow drop that Bert swung at, a fraction of a second too late. "Strike," called the umpire, and the hostile fans yelled delightedly. The next one Bert drove out for what looked like a good hit, but it turned out to be a foul. "Two strikes," barked the umpire, and some of the people in the grandstand rose as if to leave, evidently thinking that the game was practically over.

Bert watched every motion of the pitcher as he wound up, and so was pretty sure what kind of a ball was coming. The pitcher was noted for his speed, and, almost at the moment the ball left his hand, Bert swung his bat straight from the shoulder, with every ounce of strength he possessed in back of it. There was a sharp crack as the bat met the ball, and the sphere mounted upward and flew like a bullet for the center field fence.

As if by one impulse, every soul in the grandstand and bleachers rose to his or her feet, and a perfect pandemonium of yells broke forth. The fielders sprinted madly after the soaring ball, but they might have saved themselves the trouble. It cleared the fence by a good ten feet, and Bert cantered leisurely around the bases, and came across the home plate with the winning run.

Then a yelling, cheering mob swept down on the field, and enveloped the players. In a moment Bert and some of the others were hoisted up on broad shoulders, and carried around the field by a crowd of temporary maniacs. It was some time before Bert could get away from his enthusiastic admirers, and join the rest of his teammates.

As he entered the dressing rooms, Reddy grasped his hand, and said, "Wilson, you have done some great work to-day, and I want to congratulate you. From now on you are one of the regular team pitchers."

"Thank you, sir," replied Bert, "but I don't deserve any special credit. We all did the best we could, and that was all anybody could do."

So ended the first important game of the season, and Bert's position in the college was established beyond all question. Winters' friends made a few half-hearted efforts to detract from his popularity, but were met with such a cold reception that they soon gave up the attempt, and Bert was the undisputed star pitcher of the university team.

CHAPTER VI

THE FIRE

"Gee whiz! I'm glad I don't have to do this every day," said Tom, as he stood, ruefully regarding his trunk, whose lid refused to close by several inches.

"I'm jiggered if I see why it should look like that. Even with the fellows' things, it isn't half as full as it was when I came from home, and it didn't cut up like that."

The Easter holidays were approaching, and "the three guardsmen" had received a most cordial invitation from Mr. Hollis to spend them with him at his home.

Feeling the strain of the baseball season, the fellows were only too glad of a short breathing spell and had gratefully accepted the invitation. They were looking forward with eager anticipation to the visit.

They would not need very much luggage for just a few days' stay, so, as Tom owned a small steamer trunk, they had decided to make it serve for all three. The fellows had brought their things in the night before and left Tom to pack them.

Tom had heard people say that packing a trunk was a work of time, and had congratulated himself on the quickness and ease with which that particular trunk was packed; but when he encountered the almost human obstinacy with which that lid resisted his utmost efforts, he acknowledged that it wasn't "such a cinch after all."

After one more ineffectual effort to close it, he again eyed it disgustedly.

"I can't do a blamed thing with it," he growled, and then catching the sound of voices in Dick's room overhead, he shouted:

"Come on in here, fellows, and help me get this apology for a trunk shut."

When Dick and Bert reached him, Tom was stretched almost full length on the trunk and raining disgusted blows in the region of the lock.

He looked so absurdly funny that the fellows executed a war dance of delight and roared with laughter, and then proceeded to drag Tom bodily off the trunk.

Landing him with scant ceremony on the floor, they proceeded to show the discomfited Freshman that a trunk lid with any spirit could not consent to close over an indiscriminate mixture of underwear, pajamas, suits of clothes, collar boxes, and shoe and military brushes—most of these latter standing upright on end.

With the brushes lying flat, boxes stowed away in corners, and clothing smoothly folded, the balky trunk lid closed, as Tom, grinning sheepishly, declared, "meeker a hundred times than Moses."

This disposed of, and dressed and ready at last, their thoughts and conversation turned with one accord to the delightful fact that Mr. Hollis was to send the old "Red Scout" to take them to his home.

The very mention of the name "Red Scout" was sufficient to set all three tongues going at once, as, during the half-hour before they could expect the car, they recalled incidents of that most glorious and exciting summer at the camp, when the "Red Scout" had been their unending source of delight.

"Do you remember," said Tom, "the first time we went out in her, when we were so crazy with the delight of it that we forgot everything else, and gave her the speed limit, and came near to having a once-for-all smash-up?"

They certainly did. "And," said Dick, "the day we gave poor old Biddy Harrigan her first 'artymobile' ride. Didn't she look funny when the wind spread out that gorgeous red feather?"

They all laughed heartily at this recollection, but their faces grew grave again as they recalled the time when, the brake failing to work, they rushed over the bridge with only a few inches between them and disaster.

"That certainly was a close call," said Bert, "but not so close as the race we had with the locomotive. I sure did think then that our time had come."

"But," Tom broke in, "'all's well that ends well,' and say, fellows, did it end well with us? Will you ever forget that wonderful race with the 'Gray Ghost'? Great Scott! I can feel my heart thump again as it did that final lap. And that last minute when the blessed old 'Red Scout' poked her nose over the line—ahead!" and in his excitement Tom began forging around the room at great speed, but made a rush for the window at the sound of a familiar "toot, to-oo-t."

"There she is," he announced joyfully, and, taking the stairs three steps at a time, and crossing the campus in about as many seconds, they gave three cheers for the old "Red Scout," which bore them away from college scenes with its old-time lightning speed.

Easter was late that year and spring had come early. There had been a number of warm days, and already the springing grass had clothed the earth in its Easter dress of soft, tender green. Tree buds were bursting into leaf, and in many of the gardens that they passed crocuses were lifting their little white heads above the ground. Robins flashed their red and filled the air with music. Spring was everywhere! And, as the warm, fragrant air swept their faces they thrilled with the very joy of living, and almost wished the ride might last forever.

At last, "There is Mr. Hollis' house, the large white one just before us," said the chauffeur, and, so swiftly sped the "Red Scout" that almost before the last word was spoken, they stopped and were cordially welcomed by Mr. Hollis.

As they entered the hall they stood still, looked, rubbed their eyes and looked again. Then Tom said in a dazed way, "Pinch me, Bert, I'm dreaming." For there in a row on either side of the hall stood every last one of the fellows who had camped with them that never-to-be-forgotten summer. Bob and Frank and Jim Dawson, Ben Cooper and Dave and

Charlie Adams, and—yes—peeping mischievously from behind the door, Shorty, little Shorty! who now broke the spell with:

"Hello, fellows. What's the matter? Hypnotized?"

Then—well it was fortunate for Mr. Hollis that he was used to boys, and so used also to noise; for such a shouting of greetings and babel of questions rose, that nobody could hear anybody else speak. Little they cared. They were all together once more, with days of pure pleasure in prospect. Nothing else mattered; and Mr. Hollis, himself as much a boy at heart as any one of them, enjoyed it all immensely.

Glancing at the clock, he suddenly remembered that dinner would soon be served, and drove the three latest arrivals off to their room to prepare.

Short as the ride had seemed to the happy automobilists, it had lasted several hours. Though they had eaten some sandwiches on the way, they were all in sympathy with Tom who, while they prepared for dinner confided to his chums that he was a "regular wolf!"

It goes without saying that they all did ample justice to that first dinner, and that there never was a jollier or more care-free company. None of the boys ever forgot the wonderful evening with Mr. Hollis.

A man of large wealth and cultivated tastes, his home was filled with objects of interest. He spared no pains to make his young guests feel at home and gave them a delightful evening.

The pleasant hours sped so rapidly that all were amazed when the silvery chimes from the grandfather's clock in the living room rang out eleven o'clock, and Mr. Hollis bade them all "good-night."

They had not realized that they were tired until they reached their rooms. Once there, however, they were glad to tumble into their comfortable beds, and, after a unanimous vote that Mr. Hollis was a brick, quiet reigned at last.

To Bert in those quiet hours came a very vivid dream. He thought he was wandering alone across a vast plain in perfect darkness at first, in which he stumbled blindly forward.

Suddenly there came a great flash of lightning which gleamed for a moment and was gone. Instantly there came another and another, one so closely following the other that there was an almost constant blinding glare, while all the while the dreamer was conscious of a feeling of apprehension, of impending danger.

So intense did this feeling become and so painful, that at last the dreamer awoke — to find that it was not all a dream! The room was no longer dark and he saw a great light flashing outside his window pane. Springing from bed it needed only one glance to show him that the wing of the neighboring house only a few hundred feet away was in flames.

Giving the alarm, and at the same time pulling on a few clothes, he rushed out of the house and over to the burning building. So quick was his action that he had entered into the burning house and shouted the alarm of fire before Mr. Hollis and his guests realized what was happening. Very soon all the inmates of Mr. Hollis' house and of the neighboring houses rushed to the scene to do what they could, while awaiting the arrival of the local fire engines.

In the meantime Bert had stopped a screaming, hysterical maid as she was rushing from the house and compelled her to show him where her mistress slept. The poor lady's room was in the burning wing and Bert and Mr. Hollis, who had now joined him, broke open the door. They found her unconscious from smoke and, lifting her, carried her into the open air.

Nothing could be learned from the maids. One had fainted and the other was too hysterical from fright to speak coherently. One of the neighbors told them that the owner was away on business and not expected home for several days. He asked if the child were safe, and just at that moment the little white-clad figure of a child about six years old appeared at one of the upper gable windows.

By this time, though the engines had arrived, and were playing streams of water on the burning building, the fire had spread to the main house and both the lower floors were fiercely burning. Entrance or escape by the stairways was an impossibility, and the longest ladders reached barely to the second story windows. The local fire company was not supplied with nets.

It seemed to all that the little child must perish, and, to add to the horror of the scene, the child's mother had regained consciousness, and, seeing her little one in such mortal danger, rushed frantically toward the burning house. She was held back by tender but strong hands. She could do nothing to help her child, but her entreaties to be allowed to go to her were heart-breaking.

All but one were filled with despair. Bert, scanning the building for some means of rescue, saw that a large leader pipe ran down a corner of the building from roof to ground, and was secured to the walls of the house by broad, iron brackets. The space between it and the window where the child stood seemed to be about three feet. If he could climb that leader by means of those iron supports, he might be able to leap across the intervening space and reach the window.

All this passed through Bert's mind with lightning-like rapidity. He knew that if he failed to reach the window — well, he would not consider that.

Coming to quick decision, he ran forward, dodged the detaining hands stretched out, and before anyone had an inkling of his purpose, was climbing the ladder from bracket to bracket. More than one called frantically to come back, but with the thought of that despairing mother, and with his eyes fixed on the little child in the window, he went on steadily up, foot by foot, until, at last, he was on a level with the window. Now he found that distance had deceived him and that the window was fully five feet away instead of three.

The crowd, standing breathless now, and still as death, saw him pause and every heart ached with apprehension, fearing that he would be forced to return and leave the little one to her awful fate. Eyes smarted with the intensity with which they stared. Could he with almost nothing to brace his feet upon, spring across that five feet of wall? He could not even take a half-minute to think. The flames might at any second burst through the floor into the room in which the little child had taken refuge. He dared not look down, but in climbing he had noticed that the flames, as the wind swayed them, were sweeping across the ladders. He must decide.

His resolve was taken, and he gathered his muscles together for the spring.

Now, Bert, you have need to call upon all your resources. Well for you that your training on the diamond has limbered and strengthened your muscles, steadied your nerves, quickened your eye, taught you lightning perception and calculation and decision. You have need of them all now. Courage, Bert! Ready, now!

The frantic mother saw him gather himself together and spring to what seemed to be certain death. His fingers grip the window sill, but, as his weight drags upon them, they slip. Ah! he never can hold that smooth surface—and many turn away their faces, unable to bear the sight. But look! he is still there. His fingers desperately tighten their grip upon the sill, and now he begins to draw himself up, slowly, reaching inside the window for a firmer hold. He has his knee on the sill—and a great shout goes up from the crowd as he drops inside the window beside the child.

But their relief was short-lived, for now the same thought seized everyone. How was he to get back? He could not return the way he went up, for, even unhampered by the child, he could not make the leap back to the pipe. With anxious, despairing eyes, they watched the window from which great clouds of smoke were pouring now, mingled with tiny tongues of flame.

It seemed an hour that they had waited, but it was only a few moments before the brave fellow reappeared at the window, with the child wrapped in a blanket, strapped firmly to his shoulders. Another moment and a long woolen blanket dangled from the window sill, and with the agility of a monkey Bert began to let himself down hand over hand. With beating hearts into which hope had begun again to creep, the breathless people watched him.

But surely the flames, sweeping now up and out from the second story window will shrivel that blanket and burn it through. But they do not, for though they wrap themselves fiercely about it, they seem unable to destroy it; and now his feet touch the topmost round of the ladder. Another moment and his hands are upon it also.

Now at last the crowd bursts into cheer upon cheer. Willing hands reach up and seize the now almost exhausted young hero, and lift him and his burden to the ground.

The child, thanks to the blanket in which Bert had wrapped her, was unhurt and in a moment was sobbing in her mother's arms, that happy mother who, overcome with joy, could only strain her rescued treasure to her heart with murmured words of love and thanksgiving.

Bert's friends crowded around him with joyful congratulations, while Mr. Hollis, filled with rejoicing at his young friend's wonderful escape from death and with admiration for his fearless bravery, grasped him by the hand, saying, "I'm proud of you, Bert, I'm proud of you! You're a hero."

Bert winced at that close grip and Mr. Hollis, looking down, saw that the hands were badly burned and hurried him from the scene, the admiring fellows closely following.

The mother with her child had been taken away by kind and sympathetic friends, but not before she had thanked Bert with full heart for giving her child back to her.

No king ever held higher court or with more devoted or admiring subjects than did Bert while they waited at Mr. Hollis' home for the coming of a doctor to dress his burns. Nothing was talked of but the exciting events of the day and Bert's share in them. With faces still glowing with excitement, they lived over again all the events of the early morning, and Bert had to answer all sorts of questions as to "How he ever came to think of that leader pipe?" "What he would have done if the blanket had burned through?" and a dozen others.

"Well," Shorty summed up, "Bert sure is a wonder," to which there was a hearty assent.

The arrival of the doctor put an end to all this to Bert's great relief, for he was much too modest to enjoy being praised.

The burns were found to be not very serious, but the pain added to the great physical exertion and the intense nervous strain had brought poor Bert almost to the breaking point, and the doctor ordered him to bed.

Very gladly he settled down after so many hours of excitement with Mr. Hollis' parting words in his ears, "If I had a son like you, Bert, I should be very proud of him to-day."

He was drifting happily into dreamland when Tom poked his head inside the door and said, "You've got to answer one more question before you go to sleep, old man. What charm did you work around that old blanket you came down on from the window so that it would not burn?"

"Made it soaking wet, bonehead," came the sleepy reply, and Tom vanished.

CHAPTER VII

TAKING HIS MEDICINE

The team had been tested almost to its limit this season, and the strain was beginning to show. Each player was worked up to the highest possible nervous tension, and no man can last long under such conditions. Even with professional players this condition becomes very apparent in a hard-fought series, and so was even more plainly seen among these comparatively inexperienced contestants for the honor of their alma mater.

Another thing that tended strongly to demoralize them was the fact of Bert's being unable to play. His burned hands, while rapidly mending, were still unable to grip the ball. Of course, they knew that this was merely a temporary calamity, but even to have the pitcher on whom they had based their strongest hopes out of commission for almost two weeks meant much to them. Winters and Benson, while undoubtedly good pitchers, fell considerably short of the standard set by Bert, and all the players realized this.

Of course, it may be argued that they should not allow themselves to be affected by anything of this kind, but no one who has not actually been a ball player can fully realize what it means to a team, when they are nearing the end of a neck and neck struggle, to be deprived of their star pitcher. It must also be remembered that Bert, while not by any means as good a batter as he was a pitcher, was nevertheless a strong batsman, and had the happy faculty of "swatting them out" at the time when they would do the most good. On this account, his loss was felt more keenly than would have ordinarily been the case.

Another thing, but one that was never openly alluded to, was the knowledge that each boy had, that Winters was not the pitcher he had been once upon a time. His breaks from training were becoming more and more frequent, and all that the coach could say in the way of threat or entreaty seemed to have no effect. Winters had gotten in with a fast set, and no argument or persuasion could induce him to see the error of his way.

Reddy did not dare to remove him from the team, however, as that would have left him only one pitcher of any value, namely, Benson, and nobody knew better than the wily trainer that Benson could seldom be depended on to pitch good ball during an entire game.

Again and again Reddy had cursed the fate that deprived him of his star pitcher at such a crucial time, but of course, as is usually the case, that did little good. It was too late now to try to develop another pitcher, even had he known of anyone capable of training for that important post, which he did not.

So he just set his jaw, and resolved to make the best of what he had. Up to to-day, which was destined to see one of the season's most important battles, he had managed, by dint of skillful coaching and substituting at critical moments, to maintain the lead that the team had gained largely through Bert's remarkable work in the box.

He felt that if the team won to-day's game, they would have a comfortable lead until Bert was able to resume his pitching. If, on the other hand, they lost, he realized that they would have small chance of winning the championship. No one would have suspected from his outward appearance what thoughts were going on in his mind, but if they had, they would have been astonished. To the players, and to everybody else, he presented such a calm and composed exterior that the boys felt more confident the minute they saw him. As the time for the game drew near, he gathered the boys together in the clubhouse, and proceeded to make a little speech and give them some valuable advice.

They listened attentively, and went out on the diamond with a do-or-die expression written on their faces. Needless to say, Bert was there, and nobody felt worse than he over his misfortune.

"Gee!" he exclaimed to Tom, ruefully, "this is certainly what you might call tough luck. Here I am, with my arm feeling better than it ever did before, and just on account of a few pesky burns I can't pitch."

"It's tough, all right, and no mistake," sympathized Dick, "but never mind. If Winters can only do half way decent pitching, we'll come through all right."

Bert said nothing, not wishing to discourage his friend, but to himself he admitted that things had a rather bad aspect. The team they were to play to-day was noted for its heavy batters, and he knew that it would take a pitcher in the most perfect condition to stand the strain of nine long innings against such sluggers. His thoughts were not of the pleasantest, therefore, as he sat on the bench, nibbling a blade of grass, and watched the practice of the two teams with critical eyes.

Murray, reputed to be the heaviest hitter on the Maroon team, was knocking out flies to his teammates, and Bert was forced to admire the confident way in which he lined the ball out, without ever missing a swing.

His own team was playing with snap and ginger, though, and this fact comforted Bert somewhat.

"Well," he thought to himself, "the teams seem to be about equally matched, and if nothing out of the ordinary happens, we ought to have a good show to win. I only hope that all the rumors I've been hearing about Winters lately are not true."

As Bert had seen, both teams showed up well in the preliminary practice, and each made several plays that evoked applause from the grandstands and bleachers.

Soon the umpire walked out on the field, adjusting his mask and protecting pads, and the crowds settled down for a couple of hours of what they realized would be intense excitement.

"Battery for the Maroons, Moore and Hupfel!" shouted the umpire. "For the Blues, Winters and Hinsdale!"

As they were the visitors to-day, the Blues of course went to the bat first. They were quickly retired by snappy work and took the field. Winters seemed in fine form, and struck out the opposing batters in good shape, only one getting a hit, and he was caught stealing.

This ended the first inning, with no runs scored for either side, and Reddy began to feel more confident. However, little could be prophesiedregarding the outcome at this early stage of the game, and Reddy walked over to the bench and sat down beside Bert.

"Well, my boy," he said, "if they don't get any more hits off us than they did in that inning, we won't be so bad off, after all. Winters seems to be in fine shape, don't you think?"

"He certainly does," replied Bert, "he's holding them down in fine style. You couldn't ask for better pitching than he's putting up."

"Ye couldn't, fer a fact," said the trainer, and both settled back to see what the Blues would accomplish in their turn at bat.

Dick was next on the batting list, and he strode to the plate with his usual jaunty step. He waited two balls before he got one to suit him, but then landed out a hot grounder, and just managed to beat it to first base.

"That's good! that's good!" yelled Reddy, dancing about on one leg. "The boys are beginning to get their batting caps on now, and it won't be long before we have a string of runs longer than a Dachshund. Go to it, Blues, go to it!"

Poor Reddy! His high hopes were doomed to fall quickly. Hodge struck out, and with lightning-like rapidity the catcher snapped the ball down to second. For once, Dick was the fraction of a second too slow, and the ball beat him to the base by a hair's breadth.

"Two out!" yelled the umpire, and Reddy dropped into his seat with a dismal groan. White, the strong hitting shortstop, was the next batsman, but after knocking two high flies, he was struck out by a fast inshoot.

However, Winters appeared to be pitching airtight ball, and while a few feeble flies were garnered from his delivery, the fielders had no difficulty in catching them.

When the home team came to bat, their first man up, who happened to be the catcher, cracked out a swift, low fly between Winters and Tom, and tore around to second base before the ball came in from the field.

To Reddy's keen eyes, studying carefully every phase and mood of game and man, it was apparent that Winters' confidence was shaken a little by this occurrence. His pitching to the next batter was wild, and he finally gave the man a base on balls. Bert leaned forward intently, and his eyes were fairly glued on the players. Oh, if he could only go out there and pitch for the rest of the game! But he knew this was impossible with his hands in the condition they were, and he uttered an impatient exclamation.

With two men on bases and none out, matters began to look doubtful for the devoted Blues. The very first ball Winters pitched to the next batter was hit for a long two-bagger, and the runner on second cantered leisurely home.

Now even the fans in the bleachers realized that something was amiss with the pitcher of the Blues, and those opposed to them set up an uproarious clapping and hooting in the hope of rattling him still further. This was not wholly without effect, and Bert noted with ever-growing anxiety that Winters appeared to be unable to stand quietly in the box during the pauses in the game, but fidgeted around nervously, at one time biting his nails, and at another, shifting constantly from one foot to the other. A meaner nature than our hero might have been glad to note the discomfiture of one whom he had every reason to dislike, but Bert was not built after such a pattern. His one thought was that the college would suffer heavily if this game were lost, and he hardly gave a thought to his private grievances. The college was the thing that counted.

Winters, by a great effort, tightened up a little after this, and with the help of snappy support retired the Maroons, but not before the latter had garnered another precious run.

The visiting team did nothing, however, for although they got a runner to third at one time, he was put out by a quick throw from pitcher to first.

Thus ended the second inning, and to the casual observer it seemed as though the teams were pretty evenly matched. To Reddy's practised eye, however, it was apparent that the Blues had a little the edge on their opponents, except in the matter of pitching. Here, indeed, it was hard to tell who was the better pitcher, the Maroon boxman or Winters. Both were pitching good ball, and Reddy realized that it would probably narrow down to a question of which one had the greater staying power.

"If only we had young Wilson pitching," he thought to himself, "I would breathe a whole lot easier. However, there's no use crossing a bridge till you come to it, and I may be having all my worriment for nothin'. Somethin' tells me, though, that we're goin' to have trouble before this game is over. May all the Saints grant that I'm wrong."

For the next three innings, however, it appeared as though the trainer's forebodings were without foundation. Both teams played with snap and dash, and as yet only two runs had been scored.

At the beginning of the sixth inning, Tom was slated as the first man up, and he walked to the plate filled with a new idea Bert had given him. "Wait until about the fourth ball that that fellow pitches," Bert had told him, "and then bounce on it good and plenty. The first two or three balls he pitches are full of steam, but then, if nobody has even struck at them, he gets careless, and puts one over that you ought to be able to land on without any trouble. You just try that and see what happens."

This Tom proceeded to do, and found that it was indeed as Bert had said. The first ball pitched seemed good, but Tom let it go by, and had a strike called on him. The next one was a ball, but the third one was a hot curve that looked good, and ordinarily Tom would have taken a chance and swung at it. Now, however, he was resolved to follow Bert's advice to the letter, and so allowed the ball to pass him. "Gee, that guy's scared stiff," someone yelled from the bleachers, and the crowd laughed. It certainly did seem as though Tom had lost his nerve, and his teammates, who were not in on the secret yet, looked puzzled. Tom paid no attention to the shouts from the grandstand, and his well-known ability as a "waiter" stood him in good stead. True to Bert's prediction, the pitcher eased up a little when winding up for the next ball, and Tom saw that he shared the general impression that he had lost his nerve. The ball proved to be a straight, fast one, and Tom slugged it squarely with all the strength in his body. Amid a hoarse roar from the watching thousands, he tore around the bases and slid into third before he was stopped by White, who was waiting for him.

"Gee, Tom!" ejaculated the excited and delighted shortstop. "How in time did you ever think of such a clever trick. You sure fooled that pitcher at his own game."

"It wasn't my idea, it was Bert's," said Tom, truthfully.

"Whoever's it was, it was a crackerjack one, at any rate," said White, jubilantly. "If Flynn can only get a hit now we'll have a run, and it looks as though we would need all that we can get."

Flynn, in accordance with instructions from Reddy, laid an easy bunt down toward first base, and, although he was put out, Tom scurried over the plate about two jumps in front of the ball, and the first run for the Blues had been scored.

The small band of loyal rooters for the Blues struck up one of the familiar college songs, and things looked bright for their team. The opposing pitcher was not to be fooled again, however, and while Drake was waiting for a ball to suit him he was struck out, much to the delight of the hostile fans.

Thus at the end of the seventh inning the score stood two to one in favor of the Maroons, and their pitcher was "as good as new," as he himself put it.

Now Dick went to bat, and waited, with no sign of the nervousness that was beginning to be manifested by his teammates, for a ball that was to his liking. He let the first one go past, but swung hard at the second, and cracked out a hot liner right at the pitcher. Most pitchers would have let a smoking fly like that pass them, for fear of injuring their hands, but evidently this boxman was not lacking in nerve. The ball cracked into his outstretched mitt with a report like a pistol shot, and he held on to it.

"Out!" shouted the umpire, and Dick, who had started to sprint to first, walked to the bench with a disgusted air.

"Hang it all, anyway," he exclaimed disgustedly, "who'd have thought he would stop that one? I could just see myself resting peacefully at second base, and then he has to go and do a thing like that. A mean trick, I call it."

Dick made a pretence of taking the matter in this light manner in order to keep up the spirits of his teammates, but not by any means because he felt happy about it. Quite the contrary.

Hodge, the right fielder, came up next, but only succeeded in popping up a feeble fly that the third baseman caught easily after a short run in. White waited patiently for one to suit him, but while he was waiting, three strikes were called on him, and he retired in a crestfallen manner.

In the meantime, Reddy had been talking to Winters. "How do you feel, Winters?" he had inquired anxiously, "do you feel strong enough to hold them down for the rest of this game?"

"Aw, don't worry yourself about me," Winters had replied in a surly voice. "I'm all right. I never felt better in my life," but something in his voice belied his words.

"All right," returned the trainer, "but remember this, my lad: if we put Benson in now, we might be able to hold them down. I'm going to take your say so, though, and let you pitch the next inning. If they get to you, however, you'll have to take your medicine. It will be too late then to put Benson in, and of course Wilson is in no shape to pitch. Now, it's up to you."

"That's all right," growled Winters. Then he suddenly flared up: "I suppose if that blamed Freshie were in condition you'd have put him in to pitch long ago, wouldn't you?"

"That I would, my lad," returned Reddy, in an ominously quiet voice. "Now, go in there and pitch, and don't give me any more back talk that you'll be sorry for afterward."

Winters seemed about to make some hot reply to this, but after a moment's hesitation, thought better of it, and turned sullenly away, putting on his glove as he walked slowly to his position.

He vented his anger on the first few balls he pitched, and they went over the plate with speed and to spare. This did not last long, however, and after he had struck out one man his speed began to slacken. The second man up landed a high fly into right field that Hodge, although he made a brave try for it, was unable to get to in time. The runner raced around to third before he was stopped by the warning cries of his teammates.

"We've got 'em going! We've got 'em going!" chanted the home rooters in one mighty chorus, and Winters scowled at them viciously.

The next five balls he pitched were "wild as they make 'em," and only one strike was registered. In consequence the batter walked leisurely to first, and as he neared Winters said, "Much obliged, old chap." If looks could have killed, Winters would surely have been a murderer, but fortunately it takes more than that to kill a ball player, and so the game went on without interruption.

The following batter made a clever sacrifice bunt, and the man on third brought home a run, while the one on first reached second.

"Gee, it's all over now, I'm afraid," groaned Bert to himself. "Winters is up in the air sky high, and after their argument Reddy probably will not put

Benson in, because he's cold and it would do no good. We'll be baked brown on both sides before this game is finished."

And Bert was not far wrong. The Maroons landed on Winters "like a ton of brick," as Tom afterward said, and proceeded to wipe up the field with him. The game became a massacre, and when the home team was finally retired the score stood six to one in their favor.

When Winters came in from the field he was white and shaking, and Reddy felt sorry for him. "Just the same," he reflected, "this will teach him a lesson, maybe, and it may lead to his sticking more closely to regulations and the training table. Midnight booze-fighting and good ball playing don't mix very well." Reddy might have gone further, and said that "booze fighting" did not mix very well with anything worth while, and not have been far wrong.

Actuated by these reflections, the trainer resolved to make Winters pitch out the rest of the game, as it was hopelessly lost anyway, in the hope of making him reform.

The Blues were thoroughly demoralized by this time, and their half-hearted attempts to score met with little success. Hinsdale, after both thebatsmen preceding him had been struck out, landed on the ball for a long high fly into center, and got to second on it. He went no further, however, as Tom lifted a high foul to the opposing catcher. Of course this ended the game, as it would have been useless to finish the ninth inning.

The Maroon rooters rose in a body and rent the air with their songs and college yells. The loyal Blues present did their best, but could not make themselves heard amidst the general uproar.

"The Blues haven't got a chance for the pennant now," exulted one rooter to his friend. "They're on the downward road now, and will stay there till the end of the season. You watch and see if they don't."

But there was a Freshman pitcher on the bench that knew better.

CHAPTER VIII

SHOOTING THEM OVER

Bert and Dick and some of the other fellows were having a discussion. They had been talking on various topics, and, as was usually the case, the talk had drifted around to baseball. They had discussed the game pro and con, when Dick said:

"I wonder how fast a pitcher really can throw a ball, anyway. Of course, there's no possibility of such a thing, but it certainly would be interesting, if we could measure the speed of a pitched ball, and settle the question once and for all."

"That's easy," laughed Bert. "You just stand up there, Dick, and give me a baseball and let me hit you with it. If it kills you, we will know it was going pretty fast, but if it just cripples you, we will be forced to the conclusion that the ball wasn't traveling so very fast, after all."

"Yes, that certainly is a brilliant idea," snorted Dick, "and there is only one thing that keeps me from doing it. If, as you say, it should kill me, you fellows would have settled the question, all right, but then it would be too late for me to share in the knowledge. Therefore, I guess we'll leave the question open for the present."

"Aw, gee, Dick," laughed one of the others, "you certainly have a mean disposition. Here you are in college, and yet you evidently haven't enough of the college spirit to make a sacrifice of yourself for the general good. Besides, it doesn't show the scientific desire for knowledge that we would like to see in you, does it, fellows?" appealing to the laughing group.

Everybody seemed to think the same thing, judging from the unanimous chorus of assent to this speech, but, strange to say, Dick proved very obstinate, and refused to offer his services in the capacity of official tester.

"But seriously, fellows," said one of the boys, John Bennett by name, "I don't see why we couldn't do something of the kind. I shouldn't think it would be so hopeless, after all."

At first they thought he was joking, but when they realized that he was in earnest, a chorus of ridicule arose. Bennett refused to be hooted down, however, and finally managed to get a hearing.

"You see, it's this way," he explained: "My father, as you all know, manufactures guns and rifles of all descriptions. Now, some people with a little more sense in their noodles than you poor boobs," with a sarcastic inflection, "have asked what the speed of a rifle bullet was, and what's more, have managed to find out. Going on the same principle, I don't see why we couldn't find out the speed of a baseball."

"How do they find that out?" asked one, unbelievingly, "a rifle bullet has been known to go pretty fast at times, you know."

"You don't mean it, do you?" asked Bennett, sarcastically. "I always thought bullets crept along the ground something after the manner of snails, or something equally fast, didn't you fellows?"

"Go on, go on," they laughed, "if you've got an idea in what you call your brain, for heaven's sake get it out before you forget it. Go on and tell us how it is that they measure the speed of a bullet."

"Well, it's this way," said Bennett, "they arrange an electric wire in front of the muzzle of the gun, so that as the bullet comes out it is bound to break it. Then, the object at which the gun is aimed is also connected up by electricity. Observe, gentlemen, what happens when the gun is discharged. The bullet, as it saunters from the gun, cuts the electric wire, and by so doing registers the exact fraction of a second that this happens. When it hits the target, a similar process takes place, and then of course it is a simple matter to subtract the time the bullet left the gun from the time it hit the target, and thus, gentlemen, we arrive at the result, namely, the time it took the bullet to go across the intervening distance. I trust, gentlemen (and others), that I have made myself perfectly clear."

"Aw," spoke up one of the fellows, popularly known as "Curley," "who couldn't think of a simple thing like that. The only reason that I didn't think of it right off was that it was too easy for me even to consider."

"Oh, sure, we all understand that perfectly," replied Bennett, "but, seriously, fellows, if you would care to try the experiment, I am sure that my father would help us all he could. It wouldn't be any trick at all for him to rig up something on the same principle that would give us an accurate idea of how fast Bert, for instance, could propel a baseball through the surrounding atmosphere. Say the word, and I'll write to him about it to-night. We ought to hear from him by the day after to-morrow, at the latest."

Bert saw that Bennett was in earnest, and so said:

"It certainly would be very interesting, old man. I've often wondered just what speed I was capable of, and I don't see why your plan shouldn't be feasible. What do you think, Dick?"

"I think it would be well worth the try, at all events," replied Dick, "and say, fellows, while we were about it, Bennett's father might be willing to show us over the factory and give us an idea of how the guns are made. Do you think he would, old top?" addressing Bennett.

"Surest thing you know," responded the latter, heartily. "I know he would be glad to have you come, even if you are a bunch of bums," smilingly.

"All right, we'll consider that settled, then," said Bert. "You write to him right away, and we'll try our little experiment as soon as possible. Believe me, I'm anxious to try it. I sure would like to know."

Thus the matter was settled, and after a little more talk and speculation on the same subject, the boys dispersed to their rooms to prepare recitations for the morrow.

A day or so later, when some of them had forgotten about the proposed test, Bennett came up to the group assembled in Bert's and Dick's room, and said:

"See here, fellows! What did I tell you? I just received this letter from dad, and he says to go as far as we like. He says that he spoke of the matter to the foreman of the testing department, and he thinks our plan is feasible."

"Gee, that's fine," exclaimed Tom, who was of the group. "How long did he think it would be before he would be ready?"

"Oh, pretty near any time that we could get to the factory. Of course, it will take him a few days to rig up the apparatus, but he says he will have it ready by next Saturday, and as that is a holiday for most of us, I think it would be a good time to go. How would that suit you, Bert?"

"First rate," replied Bert, "I'll take it as easy as I can this week in the line of pitching, so that I will have full strength for the test. I'll have to establish a record," laughingly.

"I'll tell you what we can do," said Walter Harper, one of the "subs" on the team, "let's get up a race between Bert's baseball and a bullet. I think that Bert ought to beat a bullet easily."

"Well," laughed Bert, "maybe I can't exactly beat a bullet, but I'll bet my ball will have more curve on it than any bullet ever invented."

"That reminds me of a story I heard the other day," spoke up one. "The father of a friend of mine went out to hunt deer last fall. He had fair luck, but everybody was talking about a deer that had been fooling all the hunters for several seasons. It seems that this deer was such an expert dodger, that when anyone started to shoot at him he would run around in circles and thus avoid the bullet. Well, my friend's father thought over the matter for a long time, and finally hit on a plan to outwit the deer. Can you guess how he did it?"

Many were the schemes offered by the ingenious listeners, but none of them seemed satisfactory. Finally all gave up the problem, and begged the story teller to give them the explanation.

"Well," he said, "it's very simple, and I'm surprised and grieved that none of you fatheads have thought of it. Why, he simply bent the barrel of the gun around, so that when the bullet came out it chased the deer around in circles, and killed him without any trouble. Now — —" but here he was interrupted by a storm of indignant hoots and hisses, and rushed from the room amid a perfect shower of books of all descriptions.

"Gee," said Tom, "I've heard some queer hunting stories, but that one was the limit. Many a man has died for less."

"Oh, well, he's more to be pitied than scorned," laughed Dick, and they proceeded to discuss the details of Saturday's trip.

"It will be no end of fun, I can promise you," said Bennett. "It's really an education in itself to go through that factory and see the way things are done. You can bet there's no time or effort wasted there. Everything is figured down to the very last word for efficiency, and if all the world were run on the same basis it would be a pretty fine place to live in."

"List to the philosopher, fellows," said Bert. "I'm afraid Bennett's studies are going to his head, and he's actually beginning to believe what the profs tell him."

"That is indeed a sign of failing mental powers," laughed Tom. "I'm afraid that if we don't do something for our poor friend, he will degenerate until finally he becomes nothing but a 'greasy grind.' After that, of course, he can sink no lower."

"Aw, you fellows think you're funny, don't you," grunted Bennett, disgustedly, "you're such boneheads that when somebody with real brains, like myself, for instance, gets off a little gem of thought you are absolutely incapable of appreciating it."

"Fellows," said Bert, gravely, "we have made an important discovery. Bennett has brains. We know this is so, because he himself admits it. Well, well, who would have suspected it?"

This sally was greeted with laughter, but, seeing that Bennett was becoming a little angry, Bert changed the subject, and they were soon deep in details of the forthcoming trip. Dick was delegated to buy the tickets, and when all had paid in their money it was seen that twenty-four were going.

"That will just be a good crowd," said Bert. "We'll leave here on the 9:21 train, and that will take us to W — — at a little after ten. We can look over the factory in the morning, and tell Mr. Bennett how to run it," — with a mischievous glance at Bennett, "and in the afternoon, gentlemen, I will make my world renowned attempt to pitch a baseball against time. Do you think that will suit your father, John?"

"Sure, that will be all right," answered Bennett, and so the matter was settled.

The following Saturday turned out to be ideal, and everybody was in high spirits when they gathered at the station. They had to wait ten or fifteen minutes for the train, which had been delayed, but they found plenty to do in the meantime. They sang, played leap frog, and in a dozen other ways gave vent to their high spirits. Some of the passengers envied their light hearts, and remembered the days when they, too, had been full of life and fun, and the world had just been a place to be merry in.

The waiting passed like a flash, and before they knew it the train came into sight around a curve. When it drew up they all made a rush to get on, and before the train was finally started again had almost driven the conductor frantic.

"Byes will be byes, though," he grinned to himself, later on, "and be the same token, Oi don't begrudge the youngsters any of their fun, even if it did hold the thrain back a full three minutes. Have a good time while yer living, says Oi, for yez'll be a long time dead."

The train fairly flew along, as the engineer was making up for lost time, and it was not long before the conductor sang out, "W — —!" and they had arrived. They all tumbled off, and Tom, to save time, went through the car window.

"Be gorry, yez are a wild bunch of youngsters," said the old conductor to Bert. "But Oi remember when Oi was a lad Oi was the same way, so Oi fergives yez the delays and worriments yez have caused me this day. Have a good toime, and luck be wid yez."

"Thanks," laughed Bert; "won't you come along?"

"Thank ye kindly, but Oi guess Oi'll have to deny meself the pleasure, me bye," grinned the conductor, and the train drew out of the station.

"Gee," said Tom, as he gazed around, "I don't think we'll have much trouble locating the factory, Bennett. It seems to be a rather conspicuous part of the landscape."

It was, indeed. The whole town was founded on the factory industry, and practically every able-bodied man in the place worked there. The factory was an immense six-story affair, with acres and acres of floor space. All around it were streets lined with comfortable-looking cottages, in which the workmen lived. Everything had a prosperous and neat appearance, and the boys were agreeably surprised. Most of them had expected to see a grimy manufacturing town, and were quite unprepared for the clean community they saw spread out before them.

Bennett headed them straight toward the factory, but as they went along pointed out features of the town.

"You see," he explained, "the whole town is practically part of the factory. When that was established a few houses were built around it, and as the factory grew, the town grew along with it, until now it is what you see it. We have one of the biggest gun manufacturing plants in the world here," he added, proudly.

"It certainly is some class, John," admitted Bert; "it's bigger and cleaner than I ever expected it would be."

Soon they had reached the factory itself, and Bennett ushered them into the office. There they were presented to a gray-haired man whom John proudly introduced as his father, and they were made perfectly at home.

After a little talk, Mr. Bennett pressed a button, and a capable looking man appeared.

"Sawkins," said Mr. Bennett, "here are the young men for whom we've been turning the factory upside down the last few days. Just show them around, will you, and explain things to them a little."

"Certainly," acquiesced Sawkins, who was the foreman. "Step right this way, gentlemen."

The following two hours were probably among the most interesting any of the boys had ever known. The foreman started at the beginning, showing them the glowing molten metal in immense cauldrons. He was a man of considerable education, and great mechanical ability. He explained every process in words as free as possible of technicalities, and the young fellows felt that they understood everything that he undertook to explain. He showed them how the metal was cast, how the guns were bored out, the delicate rifling cut in, and a thousand other details. His listeners paid close attention to everything he said, and seeing this, he took extra pains to make everything clear to them. As he said to Mr. Bennett afterward, "It was a pleasure to talk to a bunch of men that understood what was told them."

Finally they came to the testing room, and this proved, if possible, even more interesting than what had gone before. The foreman showed them the various ranges, and some of the penetrating feats of which the rifles were capable. It was almost unbelievable.

"See this little toy?" he said, picking out a beautifully made gun from a rack on the wall. "The projectile discharged from this arm will penetrate over forty-five planks, each one seven-eighths of an inch thick. And then, look at this,"—holding up an ax-head with three clean holes bored through it—"here's what it can do to tempered steel. I don't think it would be very healthy to stand in its way."

"No, I guess it wouldn't," said Dick. "I'd prefer to be somewhere else when one of those bullets was wandering around loose."

Mr. Sawkins then showed them some photographs of bullets taken while in flight. At first sight this seems an impossibility, but nevertheless it is an accomplished fact. The method used is much the same as John Bennett has described in the early part of this chapter. As the bullet leaves the gun it cuts a wire, which in turn snaps the shutter of a very high-speed camera. The lenses on a camera of this kind are very expensive, a single lens sometimes costing five hundred dollars.

Then the foreman showed them the apparatus that they had rigged up to test the speed of Bert's pitching. After examining the ingenious arrangement the boys were lavish in their praise. Mr. Sawkins made light of this, but it was easy to see that he was pleased.

"Oh, it's nothing much," he said. "I just fooled around a little bit, and soon had this planned out. It was easy for me, because when I was a little younger I used to do a little myself in the pitching line on our local team, so I knew about what would be required."

While they were discussing this, Mr. Bennett strolled in, and asked the enthusiastic group what they thought of what they had seen so far.

"Gee," said Tom, impulsively, "it certainly is the greatest ever, Mr. Bennett. I never had any idea there was such an awful lot to know about gun-making. On thinking it over," he added, laughing, "I don't think of a single way that we could improve matters; do you, fellows?"

"You are more modest than my son, then," said Mr. Bennett, and there was a twinkle in his eye as he spoke. "Every time John comes here he has a lot of ideas that he is sure will better anything we have here at present. However, I have just been in this line for the last thirty years or so, and so, of course, have lots to learn."

"Aw, cut it out, Dad," grumbled the younger Bennett. "As far as I can find out, you've never tried any of the things I've proposed, and so how do you know how good or bad they are?"

"Well, the only objection to your plans was that they would generally have meant building a new factory to carry them out. Otherwise I have no fault to find with them," returned Mr. Bennett.

After a little further talk, Mr. Bennett insisted that the boys come home to his house for luncheon. Needless to say, they had no very strong objections to this, and were easily persuaded.

The proprietor's home was a large, comfortable mansion, and the good cheer offered within carried out the impression received without. There was an abundance of good fare, and the young fellows rose from the table at last with a satisfied air.

Mr. Bennett had quite a long talk with Bert during the progress of the meal, and seemed very much interested in him. It turned out that Mr. Bennett was quite a baseball enthusiast himself, so he entered heartily into Bert's enthusiasm over the game.

"I used to be quite some player myself when I was your age," he told Bert, "only I used to play a different position. I usually played catcher, and was on my team at H— —. In those days we never bothered with catcher's mitts, however, and we catchers worked with bare hands. Once I was catching in this manner, and a ball caught my thumb and half tore it off. I was so excited at the time, though, that I never noticed it, until one of my teammates noticed blood on the ball and called my attention to it. After that, when my thumb healed, you may be sure I caught with a glove. You can see the scar still," and he showed the boys the scar of what had evidently been a nasty wound.

"Well, boys," he said, at the conclusion of this narrative, "what do you say if we go on back to the factory and make that test of young Wilson's speed. I am very much interested, I assure you."

Of course there were no objections raised to this, and after a pleasant walk they arrived again at the factory. They proceeded directly to the testing room, and Bert shed his coat and vest.

"Come ahead, Dick; you catch for me until I warm up, will you?" he said, and Dick ran to the requisite distance and donned a catcher's mitt that he had brought along for the purpose. Bert pitched him a few easy balls, and then began to work up a little speed. As he shot them to Dick with ever-increasing pace, Mr. Bennett's face lighted up with interest, and finally he said, "Say, just let me try catching a few, will you, Trent? It's a long time since I've had a catcher's mitt on, but I'd like to take a try at it just for the fun of the thing."

"Certainly," responded Dick, promptly, and handed his glove to Mr. Bennett. The latter donned it quickly, and punched it a few resounding blows to "put a hole in it." "All right, my boy," he said, when the glove was prepared to his satisfaction. "Shoot 'em over, and don't be afraid to put some speed into 'em. You can't send them too fast to suit me."

Bert sent over a few easy ones at first, just to see how Mr. Bennett would handle them. The latter caught the offerings in a practised manner, and said, "Come on, young man, put some whiskers on the ball. That wasn't the best you could do, was it?"

Bert made no answer to this, but on his next pitch his arm swung around like a flail, and the ball left his hand as though propelled by a catapult. The factory owner managed to catch the ball, but he wrung his hand. "Ouch!" he exclaimed, "that ball stung my hand pretty hard right through the glove."

Young Bennett laughed in unholy glee, and danced about first on one foot and then on the other. "That's one on you, dad," he crowed; "but you ought to feel lucky that you even caught the ball. If Bert wanted to, he could pitch a ball that you couldn't even touch. Give him a fadeaway, Bert."

"Fadeaway, you say," grunted his father. "There never was a pitcher yet that could pitch a ball that I couldn't even touch. Give me a sample of this wonderful ball, Wilson."

"All right, sir," said Bert, and grinned. He wound up in the old familiar way that the boys knew so well, and shot over a ball that Mr. Bennett figured was a "cinch." He held his glove in what he thought was the proper place, but at the last moment the ball dropped abruptly and swung under the glove, missing it by several inches.

"Well, I'll be hanged," muttered Mr. Bennett, gazing stupidly at his glove. He soon recovered himself, however, and handed the glove back to Dick. "You've certainly got a wonderful ball there, Wilson," he said. "You fooled me very neatly, and I have no excuse to offer." Which showed the fellows that Mr. Bennett was a "good sport."

Pretty soon Bert announced himself as ready for the speed test, and Mr. Bennett led the way over to what looked like an empty hoop, but which, upon closer inspection, was seen to be crossed and recrossed by a web of fine, hairlike wires.

"These wires are so connected," explained Mr. Bennett, "that no matter where the ball goes, provided, of course, that it goes somewhere inside the hoop, it will break a wire, and the exact second will be recorded. Then, there is another hoop fifty feet away," pointing to a similar contrivance nearer the other end of the testing room, "and all you have to do, Wilson, is to pitch the ball through both hoops. That back hoop is a good deal bigger than any catcher's glove, so you oughtn't to have any difficulty doing it. Do you think you can manage that all right?"

"Why, I guess I can do that," replied Bert, and took up his position about eight or ten feet this side of the front hoop. Dick tossed him the ball, and Bert fitted it carefully in his hand. Then he drew his arm back as far as possible, and a second later the ball shot from his fingers at a terrific pace. It struck almost the exact center of the first hoop, parting the fragile wires as though they had been so many cobwebs, and shot through the second hoop about a foot from its edge.

"Good shot!" exclaimed Mr. Bennett, and he and the foreman hurried to the recording instruments, and started figuring up the time.

"Gee, Bert," said Tom, "I don't think I ever saw you pitch a faster ball, even when the team has been in a tight place in the ninth inning. I'd almost swear I saw it smoke as it went through the air."

"Well, fast or slow, it was the best I could do, anyway," said Bert, "so there's no use worrying about it."

In a short time, Mr. Bennett and the foreman had arrived at a result, and hurried over to where the boys were discussing the probable outcome of the test.

"You sent that ball at the rate of 114 feet a second, which is equivalent to about eighty-three or eighty-four miles an hour!" he exclaimed. "In other words, you could throw a ball after the Twentieth Century express traveling at its average speed and overtake it. As you probably know, any object traveling at a speed of a mile a minute traverses eighty-eight feet in one second, and it is on this that we have based our calculations."

"Say, Bert, that certainly was going some," said Dick, proudly, and the others were not far behind in congratulating our hero on his truly astonishing performance. It is safe to say that few professional pitchers could better Bert's record.

After the excitement had died down somewhat, John Bennett proposed that they have a shooting contest, and his idea met with instant approval. John had had unlimited facilities for perfecting himself in this art since a boy, however, and outclassed any of the others both at long and short-distance shooting.

When they had grown tired of this, it was growing late, and Bert proposed that they return. Needless to say, nobody wanted to go, but they had no choice, and so proceeded to take their leave. They all thanked their host heartily, also the good-natured and obliging foreman.

Mr. Bennett shook Bert's hand last of all, and as he ushered them to the door, said, "I'm going to take a holiday and see the next big game in which you pitch, Wilson. I'm quite anxious to see you in action."

"We'll all be glad to see you, I'm sure," returned Bert, "and nothing would give me greater pleasure than to show you over the college after the game."

"Much obliged," replied Mr. Bennett, and watched the laughing, singing group until it was hidden by a turn in the road.

The return journey seemed much longer than it had that morning, but they arrived at last, and voted it one of the best days they had ever known. The news of Bert's feat soon spread over the campus, and when it reached Reddy's ears, he nodded his head sagely.

"Just make believe I don't know a crack pitcher when I see one," he grinned to himself.

CHAPTER IX

A GALLANT RESCUE

"Say, fellows, what have you got on hand for to-day?" asked Tom, as he burst into the "sanctum-sanctorum," as Bert and Dick called their room, and sank into an easy chair.

"Nothing," said Bert, turning from a not too promising survey of the surrounding country, "absolutely and emphatically nothing! This promises to be one of the slowest days in my short and brilliant career — —"

"Hear, hear!" cried Tom from the depths of his chair. "That's fine for a starter, old top. Keep it up and perhaps you can actually persuade us that you amount to something. It's rather a hopeless task, but it wouldn't do any harm to try."

"You're such a bonehead that you don't recognize real worth when you see it," Bert retorted, good-naturedly. "There's another one," he added, pointing to Dick, who was trying to figure out a calculus problem. "He prefers grinding in calculus to listening to an interesting tale of my trials and tribulations."

"It isn't a question of preference, it's a case of dire necessity," Dick sighed, despondently. "If only I hadn't cut class the other day I would be all right, but as it is I'll have to cram to make up for it. Oh, if I only had the fellow who invented calculus here, I'd — —" and in the absence of anything better Dick pulled his own mop of tangled hair and applied himself furiously to the solving of what he called "an unsolvable problem."

"Poor old chap, never mind," consoled Tom. "When I come back to-night with old Pete under my arm I'll tell you just how I caught him."

"Do you mean to say that you are going fishing for old Pete to-day?" Dick asked, forgetting all about calculus in his excitement.

"Sure," Tom replied, placidly. "Didn't we agree that the first clear Saturday we had off we'd take for our fishing trip?"

"So we did, but that was so long ago that I'd clean forgotten it. Why didn't you remind us of it sooner, Tom? You would have spared me a lot of useless worry as to how I was going to spend a baseball-less day."

"I didn't think of it myself until I came into the room," Tom admitted, "but I suppose Dick can't go with us now. It's too bad he cut the other day," he added, with a sly glance at the discarded calculus.

"Don't let it worry you," Dick retorted. "Do you suppose that anything in earth could keep me from hunting Old Pete to-day, now that you have brought him so forcibly to my mind? Go on down and get your tackle, Tom. Bert and I will join you in no time."

"But, really, Dick," Tom protested, with mock severity, "don't you realize that duty — —"

"Get out before I put you out," roared Dick, making a dash for Tom, who promptly disappeared through the door.

"Since you insist," laughed the fugitive through the keyhole, "meet me on the campus in half an hour."

"We'll be there with bells on," said Bert and Dick with one voice, and at once began their preparations for the trip.

As Dick put the calculus back on the shelf, he said, half apologetically, "I'll see you to-night, old fellow."

Half an hour later, the trio were swinging rapidly down the road, carrying their fishing poles and tackle. This was an outing that they had planned for early in the season, but up to this time they had had no opportunity to carry it out. Nearly every Saturday they had had extra baseball practice, or something unexpected had come up, but now at last they had their chance and were only too anxious to take advantage of it. Besides them was Pete.

Old Pete was a huge pickerel who was sly and wary beyond the general run of fishes. Many a confident angler had come to the lake, absolutely certain of his ability to land the big fellow, only to return, sheepish and crestfallen, to acknowledge his defeat.

So it was no wonder that our fellows were excited at the prospect of a game of hide-and-seek with the biggest and most cunning of the pickerel family.

"Just think," Bert was saying, "what it will mean if we land him. Almost all the other fellows in college have tried it without success, and if we could manage to bring back Old Pete we would be popular heroes."

"I know, but there's not much chance of that," Tom sighed. "If old Si Perkins couldn't catch him napping, I'm afraid we can't."

"Never say die, Tom," Dick said, gaily. "A day like this makes you feel equal to anything."

"So say I," Bert added, heartily. "Say, do you see that mill in front of us? Well, that belongs to Herr Hoffmeyer, and it's one of the classiest little mills I ever saw."

"It sure is working some, but where do they get the power?" Dick asked.

"Why, there's a dam right back of the mill. You can't see it from here, but when we get a little nearer I'll point it out to you. See," he added, as they neared the mill, "isn't that a great arrangement. Alongside the mill there is a narrow, deep sluice. In this is arranged a large paddle wheel and, as the water rushes through, it acts on the paddles and turns the wheel. By a system of cogs the power is then transmitted to the grinding stone."

"That sure is fine," said Tom. "I don't know that I have ever had a chance to see a working mill at such close range. Just look how the water rushes through that sluice. I wouldn't like to get in the way."

"Nor I," said Dick. "The current must be very strong the other side of the dam."

"You bet your life it is. If anybody should get caught in it, I wouldn't give that," snapping his fingers, "for his chance of life."

At this moment a bald-headed, red-faced man appeared at the door of the mill. He regarded the boys with a broad smile on his face as he carefully dusted his hands on his white apron.

"Goot morning, young shentlemens," he said, affably. "Fine morning, fine morning, fine morning," and after each repetition of this sentiment he shook his head vigorously and his smile became broader.

"It is, indeed, sir," Bert said. "We stopped for a moment to see your mill in operation. It's a very fine mill," he added.

"Yah, yah," the big miller assented, cheerfully, "it's a very goot mill. For over five year now by me it has worked. Von't you step on the insides for a minute, young shentlemens?"

"Sure thing," said Tom. "Come on, fellows. It isn't often you get a chance to see a real mill working. Old Pete can wait, I guess," and so, led by the good-natured Herr Hoffmeyer, the trio entered the mill.

For the better part of an hour they wandered around to their hearts' content. The miller showed the working of the mill wheels, and led the way into every nook and cranny, explaining as they went.

At last, when they had seen everything there was to be seen, the boys thanked their host heartily, and started on their way once more. Before they rounded a bend in the road, they turned for a last look at the mill. At the door stood their erstwhile host, honest, round face shining like the moon, while the rays of the sun glanced off in little golden darts from the smooth surface of his bald head.

"Well, that was some adventure," Bert exclaimed. "I've always wanted to see the inside of a mill, and now I've realized my heart's desire."

"I like Herr Hoffmeyer, too," Tom said, "even if I did think he was a trifle weak in the head at first. Isn't this the pickerel stream?" he asked, a minute later.

"Yes, but the fellows say that the big pickerel is further down the stream. Come along." With these words, Bert led them down the bank until they reached a shady spot, shaded by spreading trees, and carpeted with green and velvety moss.

"This place looks good to me," said Dick; "let's camp here."

"I guess this ought to be about right," Bert agreed.

In a few minutes the reels were fixed, the hooks were baited, and the lines were lowered carefully into the clear depths of the stream.

"This is what you might call comfort," said Tom, as he leaned lazily against a convenient tree.

"Bet your life," Bert agreed.

"Now, if Pete will only consent to come along and get the hook, like any other respectable, right-minded fish, my contentment would be absolute."

"Huh," Tom grunted sarcastically. "He'd be likely to do that, wouldn't he, especially if you keep up this gabfest?"

"I guess a little polite conversation won't scare that wary old reprobate. I imagine he's heard so much conversation that couldn't be called exactlypolite, especially when he calmly detaches the bait from the hook without stopping to leave his card, that he wouldn't mind our talk at all."

"Shut up," said Tom, in a low voice, "I've got a bite, and the line's pulling hard."

Then, amid a breathless silence, Tom gave a quick, experienced pull to the line, and landed—not the renowned old Pete, but a small-sized sunfish, that wriggled and twisted desperately in its efforts to get away.

At this minute Bert happened to glance at Tom's face, and the look he found there was so eloquent of absolute dismay and chagrin, that he burst into a shout of uncontrollable laughter, in which Dick joined him.

"That was sure one on you, old man," he said, when he had breath enough.

"Humph," Tom grunted, disgustedly, "it sure was a sell. I thought I had old Pete cinched that time. However," he added, "I don't see that you fellows have much to say. You haven't even caught a sunfish."

"Not so you could notice it," Dick agreed cheerfully. "There's plenty of time yet, though, and all things come to him who waits. I'm right on the job, when it comes to waiting."

Bert, who had been thinking his own thoughts, suddenly broke into the conversation with an irrelevant "Say, fellows, did you ever hear the story of the man who went for a sail on a windy day — —"

"And a man coming out of the cabin asked him," Tom broke in, "if the moon had come up yet, and he answered, 'No, but everything else has'? Yes, we've heard that old chestnut cracked before."

"Well, it just struck me," Bert mused, "that it fitted your case pretty well."

"I suppose it does, in a way," Tom admitted, "but you just wait and see if I don't land that old rascal before night."

"Go in and win, my boy, and take my blessing. It doesn't make much difference who does the catching so long as he is caught," Dick said, and once more leaned his broad back against the tree with a sigh of content.

But into Tom's head had come a scheme, and he determined to carry it out at the very first opportunity. For a long time the trio sat on the grassy bank, listening to the myriad indescribable sounds of spring. They watched the gorgeous butterfly as it winged its lazily graceful way from blossom to blossom, and heard the buzzing of the bee as it invaded the heart of flowerland, and stole its nectar. The perfumed air, hot from the touch of the sun, stole upon their senses, and made them delightfully lazy.

Suddenly, Bert gave a jerk to his line and landed a fair-sized pickerel. Their luck had changed, and in a short time they had a very good mess of fish. But the great pickerel seemed farther from showing himself than ever.

Tom landed the next fish, but, instead of taking it off the hook, he threw the line, fish, and all back into the water.

"What's that for?" Dick asked. "We have plenty of bait left, and there's no use in wasting a perfectly good fish."

"Wait," Tom remarked, laconically.

They had not long to wait, however, for in a few minutes there was another jerk on Tom's line.

"Catch hold, fellows," Tom cried, "and help me pull. Gee, I can't hold it, much less pull it in."

Intensely excited, Dick added his strength to Tom's and pulled hard.

"Pull, pull!" Tom cried, almost crazy with excitement. "We can't lose him now. Come on! Come on! — now!"

And with one concerted effort they pulled the line up, falling over one another in their attempt to keep their balance. And there, at their feet, was the largest pickerel they had ever seen — old Pete. Quick as a flash, Tom landed on the prize, just in time to keep it from slipping back into the water.

"Look at him, look at him, fellows!" Tom shouted. "Here's old Pete, the biggest pickerel in the world, the wary old codger that has defied every fisherman for miles around, and has even eluded the deadly machinations of Si Perkins. Don't stand there like wooden statues — come here and help me unhook this old reprobate. Why don't you say something?"

"For the very good reason," Bert answered, drily, "that you haven't given us a chance. And for the second reason, I am so dazed I can't realize our good fortune."

"Our good fortune," Tom repeated, scornfully. "You mean my brains and common sense. Who thought of putting that fish back into the water to fool old Pete, I'd like to know?"

"You did, and we are perfectly willing to give you all the credit," said Bert. "The really important thing is that he's caught. I can hardly believe it yet. Isn't he a beauty?" he added, enthusiastically. "Look at the length of him, and the thickness — — Say, fellows, I bet we could feed the whole college on him for a month."

"I shouldn't wonder," Bert laughed. "I, for one, have never seen his equal, and never expect to again."

"What's that?" Tom demanded, sharply, as a cry of terror rent the air. "Let's find out."

"It sounded further down the stream, near the mill. Come on, fellows. Hurry!" and Bert instinctively took command, as he always did in cases of emergency.

As the boys burst through the bushes further down, the cry came again, a wild call for help, and they saw a white clad figure struggling desperately against the force of the current.

With a shout of encouragement Bert plunged into the water, and with long, powerful strokes was nearing the spot where the girl had disappeared. Once more the figure rose to the surface, but Bert knew it was for the last time. The girl was terribly close to the sluice, and as Bert swam he felt the tug of the current.

Just as the girl was about to go under, Bert caught her dress and pulled her to the surface. But how, how, could he swim with his burden against the current to the bank, which seemed to him a hundred miles off!

With resolute courage he mustered his strength and began the struggle with that merciless current. One stroke, two, three, — surely he was gaining, and a great wave of joy and hope welled up in his heart. He must make it, for not only was his life at stake, but the life of the young girl dependent upon his success. But it became harder and harder to make headway, and finally he realized that he was barely holding his own — that he had to exert all his remaining strength to prevent them both from being drawn through the sluice to a cruel death below.

Desperately he strove to push against that mighty wall of water, that, like some merciless giant, was forcing him and his helpless burden, inch by inch, to destruction. In the agony of his soul a great cry of despair broke from his lips. "It will all be over soon," he muttered. "I wouldn't care so much for myself, but the girl," and he looked down at the pale face and dark, tangled hair of the girl he was giving his life to save. They were very, very close to the entrance of the sluice now, and nearing it more swiftly every moment. But what was that black object coming toward them so rapidly?

"Bert, Bert, keep up your courage. I'm coming!" cried Dick's voice. "I'll be with you in a minute. Just a minute, old fellow."

Oh, could Dick reach them in time. Bert could only pray for strength to hold on for a few minutes. He was very near them now, and shouting encouragement at every stroke. Now he was beside them, and had taken the girl from Bert's nerveless grasp. "Here, take this rope, old fellow," he cried, "put it over your head, quick. That's the way. Now let the fellows on shore pull you in."

Bert wondered afterward why he had not felt any great exultation at his sudden and almost miraculous deliverance. As it was, only a great feeling of weariness settled down upon him, and he wanted to sleep — sleep. Then the sky came down to meet the earth, and everything went black before his eyes.

"Bert, dear old Bert, wake up. You're safe. You're safe. Don't you hear me, old fellow?" a voice at a great distance was saying, and Bert opened uncomprehending eyes on a strange world.

"Hello, fellows," he said, with the ghost of his old smile. "Came pretty near to 'shuffling off this mortal coil,' didn't I? Where is — —" he asked, looking around, inquiringly.

"The girl you so bravely rescued?" came a sweet voice behind him. "And who never, never can repay you for what you have done to-day if she lives forever?"

With the assistance of his friends Bert got to his feet and faced the girl who had so nearly gone to her death with him. For the first time in his life he felt embarrassed.

"Please don't thank me," he said; "I'm repaid a thousandfold when I see you standing there safe. It might so easily have been the other way," and he shuddered at the thought.

Before the girl could answer, another figure strode forth and grasped our hero's hand in both of his.

"Professor Davis," Bert exclaimed, as he recognized one of the college professors.

"Yes, it's Mr. Davis, Bert, and he owes you a debt of gratitude he can never cancel. Bert, it was my daughter you rescued from a hideous death to-day, and, dear boy, from this day, you can count on me for anything in the world."

"Thank you, Professor; I don't deserve all this — —"

"Yes, you do, my boy—every bit of it and more, and now," he added, seeing that the strain was telling on Bert, "I think you, Dick, and Tom had better get Bert home as quickly as you can. This daughter of mine insisted on staying until you revived, but I guess she will excuse you, now. I'd ask you to take supper with us to-night, but I know that what you most need is rest. It is only a pleasure deferred, however."

As they turned to go, the girl held out her hands to Tom and Dick, and lastly to Bert. "I am very, very grateful," she said, softly.

"And I am very, very grateful that I have been given a chance to serve you," he answered, and watched her disappear with her father through the bushes.

Then he turned to Dick and Tom. "You fellows deserve more credit than I, a thousand times more," he said, in a voice that was a trifle husky.

"Huh," said Tom, "all that I did was to run to the nearest house for a rope, and all Dick did was to hand you the rope, while Professor Davis and I hauled you in."

"Yes, that's all," Bert repeated, softly, "that's all."

"Well, come on, Bert, it's time you got back to college. I guess you're about all in," said Dick, putting his arm through Bert's and starting off in the direction of the college.

"Say, you forgot something," Tom said, suddenly. "You forgot all about old Pete."

"So we did," Dick exclaimed; "suppose you go and get the fish and poles, if they are still there, and join us at the crossing."

And they did meet at the crossing, and jogged along home, their bodies tired, but their hearts at rest, while their friendship was welded still more strongly by one other experience, shared in common.

CHAPTER X

A WILD RIDE

It was a rather gloomy morning on which the team started for the college where they were to play one of the most important games of the series. If they won, they would eliminate the Grays and have only to contend with the Maroons; if they lost, all their splendid work of the season might have gone for nought.

They were a sober bunch, therefore, as they gathered at the railway station to await their train. There was little of the usual joking and horse play to be seen, but this may have been partly due to the depressing state of the weather. As the train came in sight, however, they chirked up somewhat at the thought of having something to occupy their minds, and piled aboard their special car in a little more cheerful mood. A dense, clammy fog hung low over the ground, and it was impossible to see more than a hundred feet or so into it in any direction.

The town in which they were to play to-day was almost a hundred miles distant, and so they had a considerable journey ahead of them. The train was a little behind time, and was making extra speed in an effort to catch up with its schedule. They had traversed several miles, and were relieving the monotony of the journey with jokes and riddles. As they passed over a particularly high trestle, and looked down into the dizzy void below, Sterling, the second baseman, said:

"Say, fellows, this trestle reminds me of a story I heard a little while ago. If somebody would beg me to real hard, I might be induced to tell it to you."

"Go ahead!" "Shoot!" "Let's hear it!" came a chorus of supplication, and Sterling said, "Well, if you insist, I suppose I will have to tell it to you. The scene of this thrilling anecdote is laid in the Far West, when it was much wilder and woollier than it is at present. It seems that two horse thieves had been captured by a band of 'vigilantes,' and after a trial notable for its brevity and lack of hampering formalities, they were both sentenced to be hanged. It was in a country in which there were no trees worthy of the name, and the only available place for the execution within several miles was a high railroad bridge. To this, accordingly, the 'vigilantes' conducted their prisoners, one of whom was a Swede and the other of Irish persuasion. The two were forced to draw lots to see which one should be hanged first, and, as it turned out, the Swede drew the short straw, and so was pronounced the first victim of justice.

"The noose of a stout lariat was fastened around his neck, and when everything was ready he was shoved off the bridge. As the strain of his weight came on the rope, however, the knot of the noose became untied, and the Swede fell to the rushing river below. He was not hurt much, and those on the bridge saw him swim to the bank and scramble ashore. There was no way of getting at him, so the lynchers had to satisfy themselves with many and varied oaths. The Irishman, of course, had watched the proceeding in a fascinated manner, and as the cowboys tied the rope around his neck, he said, in an imploring voice, 'For Hivin's sake, byes, tie the rope tight this time, for I can't swim a stroke.'"

Hearty laughter greeted Sterling's narrative, and the boys felt in better spirits after it.

"That reminds me of a story I heard once," began Hinsdale. "It was when I was on a visit to my uncle's ranch in Montana, and — —"

But he was interrupted by a crash that sounded as though the end of the world had come, and the car in which they were riding reared up in the air like a bucking horse. It rose almost to a perpendicular position, and then crashed over on its side. It scraped along a few rods in this position, and then came to a grinding halt.

For a few seconds there was silence, and then a pandemonium of muffled screams and cries broke forth. Bert's voice was the first to be heard in their car, and it inquired, anxiously, "Where are you, Dick, Tom, and the rest of you? Are you alive yet? Here, you, get off my neck, will you, and give me a chance to breathe."

There was a general scramble and struggle among the debris, and soon one boy after another climbed and crawled through the broken windows until finally they all stood accounted for. Many had painful scratches and bruises, but none were hurt at all seriously. Reddy, the trainer, drew a sigh of relief. "Thank Heaven for its mercies," said he, fervently, and then, "Well, me lads, get a wiggle on, and we'll see if everybody else has been as lucky as we have. From the looks of things up forward there, it's more than I dare hope."

The front part of the train, which had sustained the greatest shock of the collision, was indeed a terrible spectacle. Running full speed, the two trains had crashed into each other out of the fog before their engineers had fairly realized that anything was amiss. The locomotives were practically demolished, and one huge Mogul lay on its side beside the roadbed, steam still hissing from its broken pipes. The other engine still was on the rails, but its entire front had been demolished, and it was a total wreck. The coaches immediately back of the locomotives had been driven on by the momentum of the cars back of them, and had been partly telescoped; that is, the cars in the rear had plowed half way through before their progress was checked. To add to the horror of the scene, thin red flames were licking up from the wreckage, probably started by the coals from the engine. Many of the passengers were unable to extricate themselves from the wreckage, being pinned down by beams and other heavy articles. Their cries and supplications to be saved were pitiful as they saw the hungry flames gathering headway and eating their way toward them, and Reddy turned fiercely to the horror-stricken boys. "Here, what are ye standing around for?" he snarled. "Git back to our car and get out the axes and fire extinguishers there. You can get at them if you try. Come on; hurry!" and the trainer sprinted back toward the rear cars, followed in a body by the willing and eager boys. In less time than it takes to tell it, they returned, some with axes and some with extinguishers. The latter could make little progress against the flames, however, which by now had gained considerable headway, so the boys, assisted by such other of the passengers who were in a position to do so, proceeded to chop and dig their way to the imprisoned unfortunates. Person after person they dragged out in this manner, until they had rescued all but one man.

He was pinned down by a timber that had all the weight of one of the heavy trucks on it, and it seemed impossible that they could get him out before the fire got to him. Already they could feel its intense heat as they chopped and pulled, wrenched and lifted, in a frenzy of haste. Nearer and nearer crept the all-embracing fire, until eyebrows and hair began to singe with the deadly heat, and they were forced to work in relays, relieving each other every minute or so.

"For God's sake, if you can't get me out of here before the fire reaches me, kill me," pleaded the unfortunate prisoner, "don't let me roast here by degrees!"

"No danger of that," gasped Bert, as he swung a huge timber aside that under ordinary circumstances he would have been unable even to move. "We'll have you out in a jiffy, now."

"Come on boys, we've got to move this truck," yelled Reddy. "Here, everybody get hold on this side, and when I say pull, pull for your lives! Now! get hold! Ready?"

"Yes!" they gasped between set teeth.

"Pull!" fairly screamed Reddy, and every man and boy grasping the obstinate mass of twisted metal put every ounce of strength in his body into one supreme effort. The mass swayed, gave, and then toppled back where it had been before!

"Don't give up!" yelled Bert, frantically, as he saw some of the men release their hold and turn away, evidently despairing of accomplishing their object. "Try it again! For God's sake remember you're men, and try again! It's a human life that's at stake!"

Thus adjured, they returned to the task, and at the signal from Reddy, wrenched and tore frantically at the inert mass that appeared to mock their puny efforts.

"Keep it up, keep it up!" gritted Reddy. Slowly but surely, every muscle straining to its utmost and threatening to snap under the terrific strain, they raised the heavy truck, and with one last mad heave and pull sent it toppling down the railroad embankment.

With a wild yell they fell upon the few light timbers lying between them and the imprisoned man, and soon had him stretched out safely beside the track. On examination it proved that he had an arm wrenched and several minor injuries, but nothing fatal.

"Nothing I can say will express half the gratitude I feel toward you young men," he said, smiling weakly up into the faces of the boys groupedabout him, "you have saved me from a horrible death, and I will never forget it."

While waiting for the arrival of the wrecking crew and a doctor, the rescued man had considerable further talk with the members of the team, and they learned, much to their surprise, that he was an alumnus of their college. Their pleasure at this discovery was very great, and that of the stranger seemed little less.

"The old college has done me a whole lot of good, all through my life," he said, "but never as much as it did to-day, through her baseball team. You will hear further from me, young men."

"Oh, it was nothing much to do," deprecated Bert, "we did the only thing there was to be done under the circumstances, and that was all there was to it!"

"Not a bit of it," insisted the gentleman. "Why, just take a look at your faces. You are all as red as though you had been boiled, and your eyebrows are singed. I declare, anybody looking at us would think that you had had a good deal harder time of it than I had."

And nothing the boys could say would induce him to alter his opinion of their heroism in the slightest degree.

Soon they heard a whistle far down the track, and shortly afterward the wrecking train hove in view. It consisted, besides the locomotive and tender, of a tool car, in which were stored all kinds of instruments, jacks, etc., that could possibly be required, and a flat car on which a sturdy swinging crane was mounted. The railroad company had also sent several physicians, who were soon busily engaged in taking proper care of the injured.

In the meantime, the crew of the wrecking train, headed by a burly foreman, got in strenuous action, and the boys marveled at the quick and workmanlike manner in which they proceeded to clear the line. As is the case with all wrecking crews, their orders were to clear the road for traffic in the shortest time regardless of expense. The time lost in trying to save, for instance, the remains of a locomotive or car for future use, would have been much more valuable than either.

A gang of Italians were set to work clearing off the lighter portion of the wreckage, and the wrecking crew proper proceeded to get chains under the locomotive that remained on the tracks. It was so twisted and bent that not one of its wheels would even turn, so it was impossible to tow it away. The only solution of the problem, then, was to lift it off the track. After the crew had placed and fastened the chains to the satisfaction of the foreman, who accompanied the process with a string of weird oaths, the signal was given to the man operating the steam crane to "hoist away."

The strong engine attached to the massive steel crane began to whirr, and slowly the great mass of the locomotive rose, inch by inch, into the air. When the front part was entirely clear of the tracks, the operator touched another lever, and the crane swung outward, carrying the huge locomotive with it as a child might play with a toy. It was a revelation of the unlimited might of that powerful monster, steam.

Further and further swung the crane, until the locomotive was at right angles to the track, with its nose overhanging the embankment. Then, with the foreman carefully directing every movement with uplifted hand and caustic voice, the locomotive was lowered gently down the embankment, partly sliding and partly supported by the huge chain, every link of which was almost a foot long.

In speaking of this chain afterward one of the boys said he wished he had stolen it so that he might wear it as a watch-chain.

The engine finally came to rest at the foot of the incline, and the chain was slackened and cast off. Then the crane took the next car in hand, and went through much the same process with it. Car after car was slid down the embankment, and in an incredibly short time the roadway was cleared of wreckage. Then it was seen that several rails had been ripped up, but these were quickly replaced by others from racks built along the right of way, such as the reader has no doubt often seen.

In a little over an hour from the time the wrecking crew came on the scene the last bolt on the rail connecting plates had been tightened, and the track was ready again for traffic.

"Gee," exclaimed Tom, "that was quick work, for fair. Why, if anybody had asked me, I would have said that no train would have been able to use this roadway for at least a day. That crew knows its business, and no mistake."

"They sure do," agreed Dick, "they cleared things up in jig time. But it only shows what can be done when you go about it in the right way."

"I only wish we had had that crane when we were trying to lift the truck up," said the trainer, who had sauntered up to the group. "It wouldn't have been any trick at all with that little pocket instrument."

"No," laughed Bert. "I think that in the future I will carry one around with me in case of emergencies. You don't know when it might come in handy."

"Great head, great head," approved Dick, solemnly, and then they both laughed heartily, and the others joined in. After their recent narrow escape from death, life seemed a very pleasant and jolly thing.

But suddenly Bert's face sobered. "How the dickens are we going to get to the game in time?" he inquired. "The service is all tied up, and it will be hours and hours before we can get there."

This was indeed a problem, and there seemed to be no solution. There was no other railroad running within twenty miles of this one, and while a trolley line connecting the towns was building, it had not as yet been completed. As Tom expressed it, "they were up against it good and plenty."

While they were discussing the problem, and someone had despairingly suggested that they walk, Mr. Clarke, the gentleman whom the boys had rescued from the wreck, strolled up, with his arm neatly done up in a sling. His face looked pale and drawn, but aside from the wrenched arm he appeared none the worse for his harrowing experience.

When informed of the problem facing the team, he appeared nonplussed at first, but then his face lightened up.

"My home isn't more than a mile from here," he said, "and I have recently bought a large seven-passenger automobile. You could all pack into that without much trouble, and there is a fine macadam road leading from within a few blocks of my house to the town for which you are bound. But there," and his face clouded over, "I forgot. I discharged my chauffeur the other day, and I have not had time as yet to engage another. I don't know whom I could get to drive the car. I can't do it on account of my broken arm."

"Shucks, that's too bad," said Reddy, in a disappointed tone, "that would be just the thing, if we only had someone to run it. That's what I call tough luck. I guess there's no game for us to-day, boys, unless we think of something else."

But here Bert spoke up. "If Mr. Clarke wouldn't be afraid to trust the car to me," he said, "I know how to drive, and I can promise we will take the best care of it. I know that car fore and aft, from radiator to taillight."

"Why, certainly, go as far as you like," said Mr. Clarke, heartily. "If you are sure you can handle it I will be only too glad to let you have it. Nothing I can do will repay a thousandth part of what I owe you boys."

"You're sure you're capable of handling a car, are you, Wilson?" inquired the trainer, with a searching look. "I don't want to take a chance on getting mixed up in any more wrecks to-day. The one we've had already will satisfy me for some time to come."

"Watch me," was all Bert said, but Dick and Tom both chimed in indignantly, "I guess you don't know whom we have with us," said Tom, "why, Bert has forgotten more about automobiles than I ever knew, and I'm no slouch at that game."

"That's right," confirmed Dick. "Bert's some demon chauffeur, Reddy. Believe me, we'll have to move some, too, if we expect to get to D— — in time for the game. Why!" he exclaimed, glancing at his watch, "it's after one now, and we're due to be at the grounds at 2:30. How far is it, Mr. Clarke, from your house to D— —?"

Mr. Clarke calculated a moment, and then said, "Why, I guess it must be from fifty to fifty-five miles. You'll have to burn up the road to get there in anything like time," he said, and glanced quizzically at Bert.

"That's easy," returned the latter, "a car like yours ought to be capable of seventy miles an hour in a pinch."

Mr. Clarke nodded his head. "More than that," he said, "but be careful how you try any stunts like seventy miles an hour. I don't care about the car, but I don't want the old college to be without a baseball team owing to an automobile smashup."

"Never fear," said Bert, confidently. "You may be sure I will take no unnecessary chances. I don't feel as though I wanted to die yet awhile."

"All right," said Mr. Clarke, and proceeded to give them directions on the shortest way to reach his home. When he had finished, Reddy sang out, "All right, boys, let's get a move on. Double quick now! We haven't a minute to lose."

Accordingly the whole team started off at a swinging trot, and it was not long before Mr. Clarke's handsome residence came into view. Mr. Clarke had given them a note, which they presented to his wife, who met them at the door. She was much agitated at the news contained therein, but, after a few anxious questions, proceeded to show them where the machine was located, and gave them the key to the garage. They raced down a long avenue of stately trees, and soon came to the commodious stone garage. Reddy unlocked the doors, and swung them wide.

"Gee, what a machine," breathed Bert, and stood a moment in mute admiration. The automobile was of the very latest pattern, and was the finest product of an eminent maker. The sun sparkled on its polished enamel and brass work. But Bert had no eyes for these details. He raised the hood and carefully inspected the engine. Then he peered into the gasoline and oil tanks, and found both plentifully supplied.

"All right," he announced, after this inspection. "Pile in someway, and we'll get a move on. What time is it, Tom?"

"Just twenty-five minutes of two," announced Tom, after consulting his watch. "I hope we don't get arrested for speeding, that's all. This reminds me of the old 'Red Scout' days, doesn't it you, Dick?"

"It sure does," agreed the latter, with a reminiscent smile. "We'll have to go mighty fast to break the records we made then, won't we, old sock?" slapping Bert on the shoulder.

"That's what," agreed Bert, as he cranked the motor.

The big engine coughed once or twice, and then settled down into a contented purring. Bert threw in the reverse and backed out of the garage. He handled the big car with practised hands, and Reddy, who had been watching him carefully, drew a sigh of relief. "I guess he knows his business, all right," he reflected, and settled back on the luxurious cushions of the tonneau. The car was packed pretty solidly, you may be sure, and everyone seated on the cushions proper had somebody else perched on his lap. This did not matter, however, and everybody was too excited to feel uncomfortable.

As they passed the porch, they stopped, and Mrs. Clarke, who had been waiting to see them off, gave Bert directions on how to find the main road. "Follow the road in front of the house due south for about half or three-quarters of a mile," she said, "and then turn to your left on the broad, macadam road that you will see at about this point. That will take you without a break to D— —. Be careful of that car, though," she said to Bert, "I'm almost afraid of it, it's so very powerful."

"It will need all its power to-day," said Bert, smiling, and they all said good-bye to Mrs. Clarke. Then Bert slipped in the clutch, and the big car glided smoothly out on the road in front of the house, and in a very short time they came to the main road of which Mrs. Clarke had spoken.

"Now, Bert, let her rip," said Dick, who was in the seat beside our hero. Bert did.

Little by little he opened the throttle till the great machine was rushing along the smooth road at terrific speed. Faster and faster they flew. The wind whistled in their ears, and all who were not holding on to their caps lost them. There was no time to stop for such a trivial item, and indeed nobody even thought of such a thing. To get to the game, that was the main thing. Also, the lust of speed had entered their hearts, and while they felt horribly afraid at the frightful pace, there was a certain mad pleasure in it, too. The speedometer needle crept up and up, till it touched the sixty-mile-an-hour mark. Reddy wanted to tell Bert to slacken speed, but feared that the boys would think he was "scared," so said nothing. Bert's heart thrilled, and the blood pounded madly through his veins. His very soul called for speed, speed! and he gradually opened the throttle until it would go no further. The great car responded nobly, and strained madly ahead. The whirring gears hummed a strident tune, and the explosions from the now open muffler sounded in an unbroken roar. The passengers in the machine grew dizzy, and some were forced to close their eyes to protect them from the rushing, tearing wind. The fields on both sides streaked away in back of them like a vari-colored ribbon, and the gray road seemed leaping up to meet them. The speedometer hand pointed to eighty miles an hour, and now there was a long decline in front of them. The boys thought that then Bert would surely reduce the power somewhat, but apparently no such thought entered his mind. Down the long slope they swooped, and then—What was that in front of them, that they were approaching at such terrific speed? At a glance Bert saw that it consisted of two farm wagons traveling along toward them at a snail's pace, their drivers engaged in talk, and oblivious of the road in front of them. Bert touched the siren lever, and a wild shriek burst from the tortured siren. The drivers gave one startled glance at the flying demon approaching them, and then started to draw up their horses to opposite sides of the road. They seemed fairly to crawl and Bert felt an awful contraction of his heart. What if they could not make it? He knew that it would have been folly to apply the brakes at the terrific speed at which they were traveling, and his only chance lay in going between the two wagons.

Slowly—slowly—the wagons drew over to the side of the road, and Bert calculated the distance with straining eyes. His hands gripped the wheel until his knuckles stood out white and tense.

Now they were upon the wagons—and through! A vision of rearing horses, excited, gesticulating drivers—and they were through, with a scant half foot to spare on either side.

A deep sigh went up from the passengers in the car, and tense muscles were relaxed. Gradually, little by little, Bert reduced the speed until they were traveling at a mere forty miles an hour, which seemed quiet, safe and slow, after their recent hair-raising pace. Reddy pulled out his handkerchief and mopped his forehead, which was beaded with perspiration.

"We looked death in the face that time," he declared, gravely. "I never expected to get out of that corner alive. If we had hit one of those wagons, it would have been all up with us. For heaven's sake, Wilson, take it a little easier in the future, will you? I don't want to decorate a marble slab in the morgue just yet awhile."

Tom pulled out his watch, and found that it was after two o'clock. "We can't be far from the town now," he declared. "I'll bet that's it, where you see the steeple over there in the distance."

"That's what it is," chimed in several of the others, who had been to the town before; "we'll get there with time to spare."

The intervening mile or so was covered in a jiffy, and the car entered the town. Almost immediately they were recognized by some in the crowd, and were greeted with cheers. A couple of young fellows whom they knew jumped up on the running-board as Bert slowed down for them.

"Gee," said one, "there's some class to you fellows, all right, all right. It isn't every baseball team that can travel around the country in a giddy buzz wagon like the one you have there. Who belongs to it, anyway?"

"Oh, it's too long a story to tell now," said the trainer. "We'll tell you all about it after the game. It's about time we were starting in to practise a little."

They soon arrived at the grounds, and were greeted by an ovation. The news of the wreck had just been telegraphed in, and the spectators had been a sorely disappointed lot until the arrival of the car bearing the Blues. The news had spread over the field, and some of the spectators had started to leave, thinking that, of course, there would be no game.

These soon returned, however, and settled down to see the struggle.

It would seem as though the Blues would have little energy left after such an exciting day as they had passed through, but such is the wonderful elasticity and recuperative powers of youth, that they played one of the snappiest games of the season, and after a hotly contested fight won out by a score of four to two.

As they returned to the clubhouse after the game, they were surprised beyond measure to see Mr. Clarke waiting for them. He greeted them with a smile, and shook hands all around with his uninjured arm.

"I caught the first train that went through," he explained, "and got here in time to see the last inning. You fellows put up a cracker-jack game, and I think you are an honor to the old college. It was a wonder you did not lose. After what you have been through to-day I should not have been a bit surprised or disappointed."

They thanked him for his kind speech, and then nothing would do but that they must have supper with him at the most expensive hotel in town. Needless to say, this meal was done ample justice, and when Mr. Clarke informed them that he had hired rooms for them for the night the announcement was greeted with a cheer.

"I have telegraphed home, so nobody will be worried about you," he said. "They know you're in safe hands," and his eyes twinkled.

It was a tired lot of athletes that tumbled up to bed that night, and soon they were sleeping the deep, dreamless sleep of healthy exhaustion.

CHAPTER XI

THE NINTH INNING

The morning of the all-important day on which the Blues and Maroons were to lock horns in order that the pennant question might be finally settled dawned gloriously. There was not a cloud in the sky and scarcely a breath of wind stirring. A storm two days before had cooled the air and settled the dust, and altogether a finer day for the deciding struggle could not have been imagined.

The game was to be played on the enemy's grounds, and that, of course, gave them a great advantage. This was further increased by the fact that it was Commencement Week, and from all parts of the country great throngs of the old graduates had been pouring for days into the little town that held so large a place in their memories and affections. They could be depended on to a man to be present that afternoon, rooting with all their might and yelling their heads off to encourage the home team.

However, they would not have it all their own way in that matter, although of course they would be in the majority. The train that brought Bert and his comrades on the day before was packed with wildly enthusiastic supporters, and a whole section of the grandstand would be reserved for them. They had rehearsed their songs and cheers and were ready to break loose at any time on the smallest provocation and "make Rome howl." And, as is the way of college rooters, they had little doubt that when they took the train for home they would carry their enemies' scalps at their belts. They would have mobbed anybody for the mere suggestion that their favorites could lose.

They packed the hotel corridors with an exuberant and hilarious crowd that night that "murdered sleep" for any one within earshot, and it was in the "wee, sma' hours" when they at last sought their beds, to snatch a few hours' sleep and dream of the great game on the morrow. Not so the team themselves, however. They had been carried away to a secluded suite, where after a good supper and a little quiet chat in which baseball was not permitted to intrude, they were tucked away in their beds by their careful trainer and by ten o'clock were sleeping soundly.

At seven the next morning they were astir, and, after a substantial breakfast, submitted themselves to "Reddy's" rubdown and massage, at the conclusion of which their bodies were glowing, their eyes bright, and they felt "fine as silk," in Reddy's phrase, and ready for anything. It was like getting a string of thoroughbreds thoroughly groomed and sending them to the post fit to race for a kingdom. To keep them from dwelling on the game, Reddy took them for a quiet stroll in the country, returning only in time for a leisurely though not hearty dinner, after which they piled into their 'bus and started for the ball field.

As they drove into the carriage gate at the lower end of the field they fairly gasped at the sight that met their eyes. They had never played before such a tremendous crowd as this. Grandstands and bleachers, the whole four sides of the field were packed with tier upon tier of noisy and jubilant rooters. Old "grads," pretty girls and their escorts waving flags, singing songs, cheering their favorites, shouting their class cries, made a picture that, once seen, could never be forgotten.

"Some crowd, all right," said Dick to Bert, as they came out on the field for preliminary practise.

"Yes," said Bert, "and nine out of ten of them expect and hope to see us lose. We must put a crimp in that expectation, from the stroke of the gong."

"And we will, too," asserted Tom, confidently, "they never saw the day when they were a better team than ours, and it's up to our boys to prove it to them, right off the reel."

"How does your arm feel to-day?" asked Dick. "Can you mow them down in the good old way, if you go in the box?"

"Never felt better in my life," rejoined Bert. "I feel as though I could pitch all day if necessary."

"That sounds good," said Dick, throwing his arm over Bert's shoulder. "If that's the way you feel, we've got the game sewed up already."

"Don't be too sure, old man," laughed Bert. "You'd better 'knock wood.' We've seen too many good things go wrong to be sure of anything in this world of chance. By the way," he went on, "who is that fellow up near our bench? There's something familiar about him. By George, it's Ainslee," and they made a rush toward the stalwart figure that turned to meet them with a smile of greeting.

"In the name of all that's lucky," cried Dick, as he grasped his hand and shook it warmly, "how did you manage to get here? I thought you were with your team at Pittsburgh. There's no man on earth I'd rather see here to-day."

"Well," returned the coach, his face flushing with pleasure at the cordial greeting, "I pitched yesterday, and as it will be two or three days beforemy turn in the box comes round again, I made up my mind it was worth an all-night's journey to come up here and see you whale the life out of these fellows. Because of course that's what you're going to do, isn't it? You wouldn't make me spend all that time and money for nothing, would you?" he grinned.

"You bet we won't," laughed Dick, "just watch our smoke."

The presence of the coach was an inspiration, and they went on for their fifteen minutes' practise with a vim and snap that sobered up the over-confident rooters on the other side. Their playing fairly sparkled, and some of the things put across made the spectators catch their breath.

Just in front of the grandstand, Bert and Winters tried out their pitching arms. Commencing slowly, they gradually increased their pace, until they were shooting them over with railroad speed. The trainer and manager, reinforced by Mr. Ainslee, carefully watched every ball thrown, so as to get a line on the comparative speed and control. While they intended to use Bert, other things being equal, nobody knew better than they that a baseball pitcher is as variable as a finely strung race horse. One day he is invincible and has "everything" on the ball; the next, a village nine might knock him all over the lot.

But to-day seemed certainly Bert's day. He had "speed to burn." His curves were breaking sharply enough to suit even Ainslee's critical eye, and while Winters also was in fine fettle, his control was none too good. Hinsdale was called into the conference.

"How about it, Hin?" asked Ainslee. "How do they feel when they come into the glove?"

"Simply great," replied the catcher, "they almost knock me over, and his change of pace is perfect."

"That settles it," said Ainslee, and the others acquiesced.

So that when at last the starting gong rang and a breathless silence fell over the field, as Tom strode to the plate, Bert thrilled with the knowledge that he had been selected to carry the "pitching burden," and that upon him, more than any other member of the team, rested that day's defeat or victory.

The lanky, left-handed pitcher wound up deliberately and shot one over the plate. Tom didn't move an eyelash.

"Strike one!" called the umpire, and the home crowd cheered.

The next one was a ball.

"Good eye, old man!" yelled Dick from the bench. "You've got him guessing."

The next was a strike, and then two balls followed in rapid succession. The pitcher measured the distance carefully, and sent one right over the center of the rubber. Tom fouled it and grinned at the pitcher. A little off his balance, he sent the next one in high, and Tom trotted down to first, amid the wild yells of his college mates.

Flynn came next with a pretty sacrifice that put Tom on second. Drake sent a long fly that the center fielder managed to get under. But before he could get set for the throw in, Tom, who had left second the instant the catch was made, slid into third in a cloud of dust just before the ball reached there.

"He's got his speed with him to-day," muttered Ainslee, "now if Trent can only bring him home."

But Tom had other views. He had noticed that the pitcher took an unusually long wind-up. Then too, being left-handed, he naturally faced toward first instead of third, as he started to deliver the ball. Foot by foot, Tom increased his lead off third, watching the pitcher meanwhile, with the eye of a hawk. Two balls and one strike had been called on Dick, when, just as the pitcher began his wind-up, Tom made a dash for the plate and came down the line like a panic-stricken jack-rabbit.

Warned by the roar that went up from the excited crowd, the pitcher stopped his wind-up, and hurriedly threw the ball to the catcher. But the unexpectedness of the move rattled him and he threw low. There was a mixup of legs and arms, as Tom threw himself to the ground twenty feet from the plate and slid over the rubber, beating the ball by a hair. The visiting crowd went wild, and generous applause came even from the home rooters over the scintillating play, while his mates fairly smothered him as he rose and trotted over to the bench.

"He stole home," cried Reddy, whose face was as red as his hair with excitement. "The nerve of him! He stole home!"

It was one of the almost impossible plays that one may go all through the baseball season without seeing. Not only did it make sure of one precious run—and that run was destined to look as big as a mountain as the game progressed—but it had a tendency to throw the opposing team off its balance, while it correspondingly inspired and encouraged the visitors.

However, the pitcher pulled himself together, and although he passed Dick to first by the four-ball route, he made Hodge send up a high foul to the catcher and the side was out.

The home crowd settled back with a sigh of relief. After all, only one run had been scored, and the game was young. Wait till their heavy artillery got into action and there would be a different story to tell. They had expected that Winters, the veteran, would probably be the one on whom the visitors would pin their hopes for the crucial game, and there was a little rustle of surprise when they saw a newcomer move toward the box. They took renewed hope when they learned that he was a Freshman, and that this was his first season as a pitcher. No matter how good he was, it stood to reason that when their sluggers got after him they would quickly "have his number."

"Well, Wilson," said Ainslee, as Bert drew on his glove, "the fellows have given you a run to start with. You can't ask any more of them than that. Take it easy, don't let them rattle you, and don't use your fadeaway as long as your curves and fast straight ones are working right. Save that for the pinches."

"All right," answered Bert, "if the other fellows play the way Tom is doing, I'll have nothing left to ask for in the matter of support, and it's up to me to do the rest."

For a moment as he faced the head of the enemy's batting order, and realized all that depended on him, his head grew dizzy. The immense throng of faces swam before his eyes and Dick's "Now, Bert, eat them up," seemed to come from a mile away. The next instant his brain cleared. He took a grip on himself. The crowd no longer wavered before his eyes. He was as cold and hard as steel.

"Come, Freshie," taunted Ellis, the big first baseman, as he shook his bat, "don't cheat me out of my little three bagger. I'll make it a homer if you don't hurry up."

He jumped back as a swift, high one cut the plate right under his neck.

"Strike," called the umpire.

"Naughty, naughty," said Ellis, but his tone had lost some of its jauntiness.

The next was a wide outcurve away from the plate, but Ellis did not "bite," and it went as a ball.

Another teaser tempted him and he lifted a feeble foul to Hinsdale, who smothered it easily.

Hart, who followed, was an easy victim, raising a pop fly to Sterling at second. Gunther, the clean-up hitter of the team, sent a grounder to short that ordinarily would have been a sure out, but, just before reaching White, it took an ugly bound and went out into right. Sterling, who was backing up White, retrieved it quickly, but Gunther reached first in safety. The crowd roared their delight.

"Here's where we score," said one to his neighbor. "I knew it was only a matter — Thunder! Look at that."

"That" was a lightning snap throw from Bert to Dick that caught Gunther five feet off first. The move had been so sudden and unexpected that Dick had put the ball on him before the crowd fairly realized that it had left the pitcher's hand. It was a capital bit of "inside stuff" that brought the Blues to their feet in tempestuous cheering, as Bert walked in to the bench.

"O, I guess our Freshie is bad, all right," shouted one to Ellis, as he walked to his position.

"We'll get him yet," retorted the burly fielder. "He'll blow up when his time comes."

But the time was long in coming. In the next three innings, only nine men faced him, and four of these "fanned." His "whip" was getting better and better as the game progressed. His heart leaped with the sense of mastery. There was something uncanny in the way the ball obeyed him. It twisted, curved, rose and fell like a thing alive. A hush fell on the crowd. All of them, friend and foe, felt that they were looking at a game that would make baseball history. Ainslee's heart was beating as though it would break through his ribs. Could he keep up that demon pitching? Would the end come with a rush? Was it in human nature for a mere boy before that tremendous crowd to stand the awful strain? He looked the unspoken questions to Reddy, who stared back at him.

"He'll do it, Mr. Ainslee, he'll do it. He's got them under his thumb. They can't get to him. That ball fairly talks. He whispers to it and tells it what to do."

The other pitcher, too, was on his mettle. Since the first inning, no one of his opponents had crossed the rubber. Only two hits had been garnered off his curves and his drop ball was working beautifully. He was determined to pitch his arm off before he would lower his colors to this young cub, who threatened to dethrone him as the premier twirler of the league. It looked like a pitchers' duel, with only one or two runs deciding the final score.

In the fifth, the "stonewall infield" cracked. Sterling, the "old reliable," ran in for a bunt and got it easily, but threw the ball "a mile" over Dick's head. By the time the ball was back in the diamond, the batter was on third, and the crowd, scenting a chance to score, was shouting like mad. The cheer leaders started a song that went booming over the field and drowned the defiant cheer hurled at them in return. The coachers danced up and down on the first and third base lines, and tried to rattle Bert by jeers and taunts.

"He's going up now," they yelled, "all aboard for the air ship. Get after him, boys. It's all over but the shouting."

But Bert had no idea of going up in the air. The sphere whistled as he struck out Allen on three pitched balls. Halley sent up a sky scraper that Sterling redeemed himself by getting under in fine style. Ellis shot a hot liner straight to the box, that Bert knocked down with his left hand, picked up with his right, and got his man at first. It was a narrow escape from the tightest of tight places, and Ainslee and Reddy breathed again, while the disgusted home rooters sat back and groaned. To get a man on third with nobody out, and yet not be able to get him home. Couldn't they melt that icicle in the pitcher's box? What license did he have anyway to make such a show of them?

The sixth inning passed without any sign of the icicle thawing, but Ainslee detected with satisfaction that the strain was beginning to tell on the big southpaw. He was getting noticeably wild and finding it harder and harder to locate the plate. When he did get them over, the batters stung them hard, and only superb support on the part of his fielders had saved him from being scored upon.

At the beginning of the seventh, the crowd, as it always does at that stage, rose to its feet and stretched.

"The lucky seventh," it shouted. "Here's where we win."

They had scarcely settled down in their seats however, when Tom cracked out a sharp single that went like a rifle shot between second and short. Flynn sent him to second with an easy roller along the first base line. The pitcher settled down and "whiffed" Drake, but Dick caught one right on the end of the bat and sent it screaming out over the left fielder's head. It was a clean home run, and Dick had followed Tom over the plate before the ball had been returned to the infield.

Now it was the Blues' turn to howl, and they did so until they were hoarse, while the home rooters sat back and glowered and the majority gave up the game as lost. With such pitching to contend against, three runs seemed a sure winning lead.

In the latter half of the inning, however, things changed as though by magic. The uncertainty that makes the chief charm of the game asserted itself. With everything going on merrily with the visitors, the goddess of chance gave a twist to the kaleidoscope, and the whole scene took on a different aspect.

Gunther, who was still sore at the way Bert had showed him up at first, sent up a "Texas leaguer" just back of short. White turned and ran for it, while big Flynn came rushing in from center. They came together with terrific force and rolled over and over, while the ball fell between them.

White rose dizzily to his feet, but Flynn lay there, still and crumpled. His mates and some of the opposing team ran to him and bore him to the bench. It was a clean knockout, and several minutes elapsed before he regained consciousness and was assisted from the field, while Ames, a substitute outfielder, took his place. Tom had regained the ball in the meantime and held Gunther at second. The umpire called "play" and the game went on.

But a subtle something had come over the Blues. An accident at a critical time like this was sure to be more or less demoralizing. Their nerves, already stretched to the utmost tension, were not proof against the sudden shock. Both the infield and outfield seemed to go to pieces all at once. The enemy were quick to take advantage of the changed conditions. Gunther took a long lead off second, and, at a signal from his captain, started for third. Hinsdale made an awful throw that Tom only stopped by a sideway leap, but not in time to get the runner. Menken sent a grounder to White that ordinarily he would have "eaten up," but he fumbled it just long enough to let the batter get to first, while Gunther cantered over the plate for their first run of the game amid roars of delight from the frantic rooters. It looked as though the long-expected break was coming at last.

The next man up struck out and the excitement quieted down somewhat, only to be renewed with redoubled fervor a moment later, when Halley caught a low outcurve just below the waist and laced it into center for a clean double. Smart fielding kept the man on first from getting further than third, but that seemed good enough. Only one man was out and two were on bases, and one of their heaviest batters was coming up. Bert looked him over carefully and then sent him deliberately four wide balls. He planned to fill the bases and then make the next man hit into a double play, thus retiring the side.

It was good judgment and Ainslee noted it with approval. Many a time he had done the same thing himself in a pinch and "gotten away with it."

As Bert wound up, he saw out of the corner of his eye that Halley was taking a long lead off second. Quick as lightning, he turned and shot the ball to White, who ran from short to cover the base. The throw was so true that he could easily have nailed Halley, as he frantically tried to get back. But although White had pluckily insisted on being allowed to play, his head was still spinning like a top from the recent collision, and a groan went up from the "Blue" supporters as the ball caromed off his glove and rolled out to center. The three men on bases fairly burned up the base lines as they galloped around the bags, and when Ames' hurried return of the ball went over Hinsdale's head to the grand stand, all the bases were cleared, and the score stood four to three in favor of the home team. It had all occurred so suddenly that the visitors were in a daze, and the home nine itself could hardly realize how quickly the tables had been turned.

For a moment rage took possession of Bert. What was the matter with the fellows anyway? Why were they playing like a bunch of "Rubes"? Did they expect him to win the game all by himself? Was the victory to be snatched away just as it was within sight? Were these jubilant, yelling rooters, dancing about and hugging each other, to send him and his comrades away, downcast and beaten? Were they to "laugh last" and therefore "best"? And the fellows hundreds of miles away, gathered at this moment around the bulletin board of the dear old college — —

No! No! A thousand times, no! In a moment he was himself again — the same old Bert, cool, careful, self-reliant. He stooped down and pretended to tie his shoe lace, in order to give his comrades a moment to regain their self-possession. Then he straightened up and shot a beauty right over the plate. The batter, who had been ordered to wait and take advantage of Bert's expected case of "rattles," let it go by. Two perfect strikes followed and the batter was out. The next man up dribbled a roller to the box and Bert threw him out easily. The inning was over, and Bert had to take off his cap to the storm of cheers that came from the "Blue" supporters as he walked to the bench.

Ainslee scanned him carefully for any sign of collapse after this "baptism of fire." Where were the fellow's nerves? Did he have any? Bert met his glance with an easy smile, and the coach, reassured, heaved a sigh of relief. No "yellow streak" there, but clear grit through and through.

"It's the good old fadeaway from now on, Wilson," he said as he clapped him on the back, "usually I believe in letting them hit and remembering that you have eight men behind you to help you out. But just now there's a little touch of panic among the boys, and while that would soon wear off, you only have two innings left. This game has got to be won in the pitcher's box. Hold them down and we will bat out a victory yet."

"All right," answered Bert; "I've only used the fadeaway once or twice this game, and they've had no chance to size it up. I'll mix it in with the others and try to keep them guessing."

Drake and Dick made desperate attempts to overcome the one run advantage in their half of the eighth. Each cracked out a hot single, but the three that followed were unable to bring them home, despite the frantic adjurations of their friends to "kill the ball."

Only one more inning now, one last chance to win as a forlorn hope, or fall fighting in the last ditch.

A concerted effort was made to rattle Bert as he went into the box, but for all the effect it had upon him, his would-be tormentors might as well have been in Timbuctoo. He was thoroughly master of himself. The ball came over the plate as though shot from a gatling gun for the first batter, whose eye was good for curves, but who, twice before, had proved easy prey for speedy ones. A high foul to the catcher disposed of him. Allen, the next man up, set himself for a fast one, and was completely fooled by the lazy floater that suddenly dropped a foot below his bat, just as it reached the plate. A second and third attempt sent him sheepishly back to the bench.

"Gee, that was a new one on me," he muttered. "I never saw such a drop in my life. It was just two jerks and a wiggle."

His successor was as helpless as a baby before the magical delivery, and amid a tempest of cheers, the Blues came in for their last turn at bat. Sterling raised their hopes for a moment by a soaring fly to center. But the fielder, running with the ball, made a beautiful catch, falling as he did so, but coming up with the ball in his hand. Some of the spectators started to leave, but stopped when White shot a scorcher so hot that the second baseman could not handle it. Ames followed with a screaming single to left that put White on third, which he reached by a desperate slide. A moment later Ames was out stealing second, and with two men out and hope nearly dead, Bert came to the plate. He caught the first ball pitched on the end of his bat and sent it on a line between right and center. And then he ran. How he ran! He rounded first like a frightened deer and tore toward second. The wind whistled in his ears. His heart beat like a trip hammer. He saw as in a dream the crowds, standing now, and shouting like fiends. He heard Dick yelling: "Go it, Bert, go it, go it!" He caught a glimpse of Tom running toward third base to coach him in. He passed second. The ground slipped away beneath his feet. He was no longer running, he was flying. The third baseman tried to block him, but he went into him like a catapult and rolled him over and over. Now he was on the road to home. But the ball was coming too. He knew it by the warning cry of Reddy, by the startled urging of Tom, by the outstretched hands of the catcher. With one tremendous effort he flung himself to the ground and made a fallaway slide for the plate, just touching it with his finger tips, as the ball thudded into the catcher's mitt. Two men in and the score five to four, while the Blues' stand rocked with thunders of applause.

"By George," cried Ainslee, "such running! It was only a two base hit, and you stretched it into a homer."

The next batter was out on a foul to left, and the home team came in to do or die. If now they couldn't beat that wizard of the box, their gallant fight had gone for nothing. They still had courage, but it was the courage of despair. They were used to curves and rifle shots. They might straighten out the one and shoot back the other, but that new mysterious delivery, that snaky, tantalizing, impish fadeaway, had robbed them of confidence. Still, "while there was life there was hope," so — —

Ainslee and Reddy were a little afraid that Bert's sprint might have tired him and robbed him of his speed. But they might have spared their fears.

His wind was perfect and his splendid condition stood him in good stead. He was a magnificent picture of young manhood, as for the last time he faced his foes. His eyes shone, his nerves thrilled, his muscles strained, his heart sang. His enemies he held in the hollow of his hand. He toyed with them in that last inning as a cat plays with a mouse. His fadeaway was working like a charm. No need now to spare himself. Ellis went out on three pitched balls. Hart lifted a feeble foul to Hinsdale. Gunther came up, and the excitement broke all bounds.

The vast multitude was on its feet, shouting, urging, begging, pleading. A hurricane of cheers and counter cheers swept over the field. Reddy was jumping up and down, shouting encouragement to Bert, while Ainslee sat perfectly still, pale as death and biting his lips till the blood came. Bert cut loose savagely, and the ball whistled over the plate. Gunther lunged at it.

"One strike!" called the umpire.

Gunther had been expecting the fadeaway that had been served to the two before him, and was not prepared for the swift high one, just below the shoulder. Bert had outguessed him.

Hinsdale rolled the ball slowly back along the ground to the pitcher's box. Bert stopped, picked it up leisurely, and then, swift as a flash, snapped it over the left hand corner of the plate. Before the astonished batsman knew it was coming, Hinsdale grabbed it for the second strike.

"Fine work, Bert!" yelled Dick from first. "Great head."

Gunther, chagrined and enraged, set himself fiercely for the next. Bert wound up slowly. The tumult and the shouting died. A silence as of death fell on the field. The suspense was fearful. Before Bert's eyes came up the dear old college, the gray buildings and the shaded walks, the crowd at this moment gathered there about the bulletin — — Then he let go.

For forty feet the ball shot toward the plate in a line. Gunther gauged it and drew back his bat. Then the ball hesitated, slowed, seemed to reconsider, again leaped forward, and, eluding Gunther's despairing swing, curved sharply down and in, and fell like a plummet in Hinsdale's eager hands.

"You're out," cried the umpire, tearing off his mask. The crowd surged down over the field, and Bert was swallowed up in the frantic rush of friends and comrades gone crazy with delight. And again he saw the dear old college, the gray buildings and the shaded walks, the crowd at this moment gathered there about the bulletin——.

Some days after his fadeaway had won the pennant—after the triumphal journey back to the college, the uproarious reception, the bonfires, the processions, the "war dance" on the campus—Bert sat in his room, admiring the splendid souvenir presented to him by the college enthusiasts. The identical ball that struck out Gunther had been encased in a larger one of solid gold, on which was engraved his name, together with the date and score of the famous game. Bert handled it caressingly.

"Well, old fellow," he said, half aloud, "you stood by me nobly, but it was a hard fight. I never expect to have a harder one."

He would have been startled, had he known of the harder one just ahead. That Spring he had fought for glory; before the Summer was over he would fight for life. How gallant the fight he made, how desperate the chances he took, and how great the victory he won, will be told in "BERT WILSON, WIRELESS OPERATOR."

THE END

Milton Keynes UK
Ingram Content Group UK Ltd.
UKHW020839260624
444769UK00011B/370

9 781836 571933